I0534005

Poor Folk by Fyodor Dostoyevsky

Fyodor Dostoyevsky was born on 11th November 1821.

He was introduced to literature very early. At age three, it was heroic sagas, fairy tales and legends. At four his mother used the Bible to teach him to read and write. His immersion in literature was wide and varied. His imagination, he later recalled, was brought to life by his parents' nightly readings.

On 27th September 1837 tragedy struck. Dostoyevsky's mother died of tuberculosis.

Dostoyevsky and his brother were now enrolled at the Nikolayev Military Engineering Institute, their academic studies abandoned for military careers. Dostoyevsky disliked the academy, his interests were drawing and architecture.

His father died on 16th June 1839 and perhaps triggered Dostoyevsky's epilepsy. However, he continued his studies, passed his exams and obtained the rank of engineer cadet.

Dostoyevsky's first completed work was a translation of Honoré de Balzac's novel Eugénie Grandet, published in 1843. It was not successful. He believed his financial difficulties could be overcome by writing his own novel. The result was 'Poor Folk', published in 1846, and a commercial success.

His next novel, 'The Double', appeared in January 1846. Dostoyevsky now became immersed in socialism. However, 'The Double' received bad reviews and he now had more frequent seizures. With debts mounting he joined the utopian socialist Betekov circle, which helped him to survive. When that dissolved he joined the Petrashevsky Circle, which proposed social reforms. The Petrashevsky Circle was then denounced and Dostoyevsky accused of reading and distributing banned works. Arrests took place in late April 1849 and its members sentenced to death by firing squad. The Tsar commuted the sentence to four years of exile with hard labour in Siberia.

His writings on these prison experiences, 'The House of the Dead' were published in 1861.

In Saint Petersburg that September he promised his editor he would deliver 'The Gambler', a novella on gambling addiction, by November, although work had yet to begin. It was completed in a mere 26 days.

Other works followed but a different approach helped immensely. In 1873 'Demons' was published by the "Dostoyevsky Publishing Company". Only payment in cash was accepted and the bookshop was the family apartment. It sold around 3,000 copies.

However, Dostoyevsky's health continued to decline, and in March 1877 he had four epileptic seizures. In August 1879 he was diagnosed with early-stage pulmonary emphysema. He was told it could be managed, but not cured.

On 26th January 1881 Dostoyevsky suffered a pulmonary haemorrhage. After the second the doctors gave a poor prognosis. A third haemorrhage followed shortly afterwards.

Fyodor Dostoyevsky died on 9th February, 1881.

Index of Contents

POOR FOLK
FYODOR DOSTOYEVSKY – A SHORT BIOGRAPHY
FYODOR DOSTOYEVSKY – A CONCISE BIBLIOIGRAPHY

POOR FOLK

April 8th

MY DEAREST BARBARA ALEXIEVNA—How happy I was last night—how immeasurably, how impossibly happy! That was because for once in your life you had relented so far as to obey my wishes. At about eight o'clock I awoke from sleep (you know, my beloved one, that I always like to sleep for a short hour after my work is done)—I awoke, I say, and, lighting a candle, prepared my paper to write, and trimmed my pen. Then suddenly, for some reason or another, I raised my eyes—and felt my very heart leap within me! For you had understood what I wanted, you had understood what my heart was craving for. Yes, I perceived that a corner of the curtain in your window had been looped up and fastened to the cornice as I had suggested should be done; and it seemed to me that your dear face was glimmering at the window, and that you were looking at me from out of the darkness of your room, and that you were thinking of me. Yet how vexed I felt that I could not distinguish your sweet face clearly! For there was a time when you and I could see one another without any difficulty at all. Ah me, but old age is not always a blessing, my beloved one! At this very moment everything is standing awry to my eyes, for a man needs only to work late overnight in his writing of something or other for, in the morning, his eyes to be red, and the tears to be gushing from them in a way that makes him ashamed to be seen before strangers. However, I was able to picture to myself your beaming smile, my angel—your kind, bright smile; and in my heart there lurked just such a feeling as on the occasion when I first kissed you, my little Barbara. Do you remember that, my darling? Yet somehow you seemed to be threatening me with your tiny finger. Was it so, little wanton? You must write and tell me about it in your next letter.

But what think you of the plan of the curtain, Barbara? It is a charming one, is it not? No matter whether I be at work, or about to retire to rest, or just awaking from sleep, it enables me to know that you are thinking of me, and remembering me—that you are both well and happy. Then when you lower the curtain, it means that it is time that I, Makar Alexievitch, should go to bed; and when again you raise the curtain, it means that you are saying to me, "Good morning," and asking me how I am, and whether I have slept well. "As for myself," adds the curtain, "I am altogether in good health and spirits, glory be to God!" Yes, my heart's delight, you see how easy a plan it was to devise, and how much writing it will save us! It is a clever plan, is it not? And it was my own invention, too! Am I not cunning in such matters, Barbara Alexievna?

Well, next let me tell you, dearest, that last night I slept better and more soundly than I had ever hoped to do, and that I am the more delighted at the fact in that, as you know, I had just settled into a new lodging—a circumstance only too apt to keep one from sleeping! This morning, too, I arose (joyous and full of love) at cockcrow. How good seemed everything at that hour, my darling! When I opened my window I could see the sun shining, and hear the birds singing, and smell the air laden with scents of spring. In short, all nature was awaking to life again. Everything was in consonance with my mood;

everything seemed fair and spring-like. Moreover, I had a fancy that I should fare well today. But my whole thoughts were bent upon you. "Surely," thought I, "we mortals who dwell in pain and sorrow might with reason envy the birds of heaven which know not either!" And my other thoughts were similar to these. In short, I gave myself up to fantastic comparisons. A little book which I have says the same kind of thing in a variety of ways. For instance, it says that one may have many, many fancies, my Barbara—that as soon as the spring comes on, one's thoughts become uniformly pleasant and sportive and witty, for the reason that, at that season, the mind inclines readily to tenderness, and the world takes on a more roseate hue. From that little book of mine I have culled the following passage, and written it down for you to see. In particular does the author express a longing similar to my own, where he writes:

"Why am I not a bird free to seek its quest?"

And he has written much else, God bless him!

But tell me, my love—where did you go for your walk this morning? Even before I had started for the office you had taken flight from your room, and passed through the courtyard—yes, looking as vernal-like as a bird in spring. What rapture it gave me to see you! Ah, little Barbara, little Barbara, you must never give way to grief, for tears are of no avail, nor sorrow. I know this well—I know it of my own experience. So do you rest quietly until you have regained your health a little. But how is our good Thedora? What a kind heart she has! You write that she is now living with you, and that you are satisfied with what she does. True, you say that she is inclined to grumble, but do not mind that, Barbara. God bless her, for she is an excellent soul!

But what sort of an abode have I lighted upon, Barbara Alexievna? What sort of a tenement, do you think, is this? Formerly, as you know, I used to live in absolute stillness—so much so that if a fly took wing it could plainly be heard buzzing. Here, however, all is turmoil and shouting and clatter. The PLAN of the tenement you know already. Imagine a long corridor, quite dark, and by no means clean. To the right a dead wall, and to the left a row of doors stretching as far as the line of rooms extends. These rooms are tenanted by different people—by one, by two, or by three lodgers as the case may be, but in this arrangement there is no sort of system, and the place is a perfect Noah's Ark. Most of the lodgers are respectable, educated, and even bookish people. In particular they include a tchinovnik (one of the literary staff in some government department), who is so well-read that he can expound Homer or any other author—in fact, ANYTHING, such a man of talent is he! Also, there are a couple of officers (for ever playing cards), a midshipman, and an English tutor. But, to amuse you, dearest, let me describe these people more categorically in my next letter, and tell you in detail about their lives. As for our landlady, she is a dirty little old woman who always walks about in a dressing-gown and slippers, and never ceases to shout at Theresa. I myself live in the kitchen—or, rather, in a small room which forms part of the kitchen. The latter is a very large, bright, clean, cheerful apartment with three windows in it, and a partition-wall which, running outwards from the front wall, makes a sort of little den, a sort of extra room, for myself. Everything in this den is comfortable and convenient, and I have, as I say, a window to myself. So much for a description of my dwelling-place. Do not think, dearest, that in all this there is any hidden intention. The fact that I live in the kitchen merely means that I live behind the partition wall in that apartment—that I live quite alone, and spend my time in a quiet fashion compounded of trifles. For furniture I have provided myself with a bed, a table, a chest of drawers, and two small chairs. Also, I have suspended an ikon. True, better rooms MAY exist in the world than this—much better rooms; yet COMFORT is the chief thing. In fact, I have made all my arrangements for comfort's sake alone; so do not for a moment imagine that I had any other end in view. And since your window happens to be just opposite to mine, and since the courtyard between us is narrow and I can see you as you pass—why, the result is that this miserable wretch will be able to live at once more happily and with less outlay. The dearest room in this house costs, with board, thirty-five roubles—more than my purse could well afford; whereas MY room costs only twenty-four, though formerly I used to pay thirty, and so had to deny myself many things (I could drink tea but seldom, and never could indulge in tea and sugar as I do now). But, somehow, I do not like having to go without tea, for everyone else here is respectable, and the fact makes me ashamed. After all, one drinks tea largely to please one's fellow men, Barbara, and to give oneself tone and an air of gentility (though, of myself, I care little about such things, for I am not a man of the finicking sort). Yet think you that, when all things needful—boots and the rest—have been paid for, much will remain? Yet I ought not to grumble at my salary—I am quite satisfied with it; it is sufficient. It has sufficed me now for some years, and, in addition, I receive certain gratuities.

Well good-bye, my darling. I have bought you two little pots of geraniums—quite cheap little pots, too—as a present. Perhaps you would also like some mignonette? Mignonette it shall be if only you will write to inform me of everything in detail. Also, do not misunderstand the fact that I have taken this room, my dearest. Convenience and nothing else, has made me do so. The snugness of the place has caught my fancy. Also, I shall be able to save money here, and to hoard it against the future. Already I have saved a little money as a beginning. Nor must you despise me because I am such an insignificant old fellow that a fly could break me with its wing. True, I am not a swashbuckler; but perhaps there may also abide in me the spirit which should pertain to every man who is at once resigned and sure of himself. Good-bye, then, again, my angel. I have now covered close upon a whole two sheets of notepaper, though I ought long ago to have been starting for the office. I kiss your hands, and remain ever your devoted slave, your faithful friend,

MAKAR DIEVUSHKIN.

P.S.—One thing I beg of you above all things—and that is, that you will answer this letter as FULLY as possible. With the letter I send you a packet of bonbons. Eat them for your health's sake, nor, for the love of God, feel any uneasiness about me. Once more, dearest one, good-bye.

April 8th

MY BELOVED MAKAR ALEXIEVITCH—Do you know, must quarrel with you. Yes, good Makar Alexievitch, I really cannot accept your presents, for I know what they must have cost you—I know to what privations and self-denial they must have led. How many times have I not told you that I stand in need of NOTHING, of absolutely NOTHING, as well as that I shall never be in a position to recompense you for all the kindly acts with which you have loaded me? Why, for instance, have you sent me geraniums? A little sprig of balsam would not have mattered so much—but geraniums! Only have I to let fall an unguarded word—for example, about geraniums—and at once you buy me some! How much they must have cost you! Yet what a charm there is in them, with their flaming petals! Wherever did you get these beautiful plants? I have set them in my window as the most conspicuous place possible, while on the floor I have placed a bench for my other flowers to stand on (since you are good enough to enrich me with such presents). Unfortunately, Thedora, who, with her sweeping and polishing, makes a perfect sanctuary of my room, is not over-pleased at the arrangement. But why have you sent me also bonbons? Your letter tells me that something special is afoot with you, for I find in it so much about paradise and spring and sweet odours and the songs of birds. Surely, thought I to myself when I received it, this is as good as poetry! Indeed, verses are the only thing that your letter lacks, Makar Alexievitch. And what tender feelings I can read in it—what roseate-coloured fancies! To the curtain, however, I had never given a thought. The fact is that when I moved the flower-pots, it LOOPED ITSELF up. There now!

Ah, Makar Alexievitch, you neither speak of nor give any account of what you have spent upon me. You hope thereby to deceive me, to make it seem as though the cost always falls upon you alone, and that there is nothing to conceal. Yet I KNOW that for my sake you deny yourself necessaries. For instance, what has made you go and take the room which you have done, where you will be worried and disturbed, and where you have neither elbow-space nor comfort—you who love solitude, and never like to have any one near you? To judge from your salary, I should think that you might well live in greater ease than that. Also, Thedora tells me that your circumstances used to be much more affluent than they are at present. Do you wish, then, to persuade me that your whole existence has been passed in loneliness and want and gloom, with never a cheering word to help you, nor a seat in a friend's chimney-corner? Ah, kind comrade, how my heart aches for you! But do not overtask your health, Makar Alexievitch. For instance, you say that your eyes are over-weak for you to go on writing in your office by candle-light. Then why do so? I am sure that your official superiors do not need to be convinced of your diligence!

Once more I implore you not to waste so much money upon me. I know how much you love me, but I also know that you are not rich.... This morning I too rose in good spirits. Thedora had long been at work; and it was time that I too should bestir myself. Indeed I was yearning to do so, so I went out for some silk, and then sat down to my labours. All the morning I felt light-hearted and cheerful. Yet now my thoughts are once more dark and sad—once more my heart is ready to sink.

Ah, what is going to become of me? What will be my fate? To have to be so uncertain as to the future, to have to be unable to foretell what is going to happen, distresses me deeply. Even to look back at the past is horrible, for it contains sorrow that breaks my very heart at the thought of it. Yes, a whole century in tears could I spend because of the wicked people who have wrecked my life!

But dusk is coming on, and I must set to work again. Much else should I have liked to write to you, but time is lacking, and I must hasten. Of course, to write this letter is a pleasure enough, and could never be wearisome; but why do you not come to see me in person? Why do you not, Makar Alexievitch? You live so close to me, and at least SOME of your time is your own. I pray you, come. I have just seen Theresa. She was looking so ill, and I felt so sorry for her, that I gave her twenty kopecks. I am almost falling asleep. Write to me in fullest detail, both concerning your mode of life, and concerning the people who live with you, and concerning how you fare with them. I should so like to know! Yes, you must write again. Tonight I have purposely looped the curtain up. Go to bed early, for, last night, I saw your candle burning until nearly midnight. Goodbye! I am now feeling sad and weary. Ah that I should have to spend such days as this one has been. Again good-bye.—Your friend,

BARBARA DOBROSELOVA.

April 8th

MY DEAREST BARBARA ALEXIEVNA—To think that a day like this should have fallen to my miserable lot! Surely you are making fun of an old man?... However, it was my own fault—my own fault entirely. One ought not to grow old holding a lock of Cupid's hair in one's hand. Naturally one is misunderstood.... Yet man is sometimes a very strange being. By all the Saints, he will talk of doing things, yet leave them undone, and remain looking the kind of fool from whom may the Lord preserve us!... Nay, I am not angry, my beloved; I am only vexed to think that I should have written to you in such stupid, flowery phraseology. Today I went hopping and skipping to the office, for my heart was under your influence, and my soul was keeping holiday, as it were. Yes, everything seemed to be going well with me. Then I betook myself to my work. But with what result? I gazed around at the old familiar objects, at the old familiar grey and gloomy objects. They looked just the same as before. Yet WERE those the same inkstains, the same tables and chairs, that I had hitherto known? Yes, they WERE the same, exactly the same; so why should I have gone off riding on Pegasus' back? Whence had that mood arisen? It had arisen from the fact that a certain sun had beamed upon me, and turned the sky to blue. But why so? Why is it, sometimes, that sweet odours seem to be blowing through a courtyard where nothing of the sort can be? They must be born of my foolish fancy, for a man may stray so far into sentiment as to forget his immediate surroundings, and to give way to the superfluity of fond ardour with which his heart is charged. On the other hand, as I walked home from the office at nightfall my feet seemed to lag, and my head to be aching. Also, a cold wind seemed to be blowing down my back (enraptured with the spring, I had gone out clad only in a thin overcoat). Yet you have misunderstood my sentiments, dearest. They are altogether different to what you suppose. It is a purely paternal feeling that I have for you. I stand towards you in the position of a relative who is bound to watch over your lonely orphanhood. This I say in all sincerity, and with a single purpose, as any kinsman might do. For, after all, I AM a distant kinsman of yours—the seventh drop of water in the pudding, as the proverb has it—yet still a kinsman, and at the present time your nearest relative and protector, seeing that where you had the right to look for help and protection, you found only treachery and insult. As for poetry, I may say that I consider it unbecoming for a man of my years to devote his faculties to the making of verses. Poetry is rubbish. Even boys at school ought to be whipped for writing it.

Why do you write thus about "comfort" and "peace" and the rest? I am not a fastidious man, nor one who requires much. Never in my life have I been so comfortable as now. Why, then, should I complain in my old age? I have enough to eat, I am well dressed and booted. Also, I have my diversions. You see, I am not of noble blood. My father himself was not a gentleman; he and his family had to live even more plainly than I do. Nor am I a milksop. Nevertheless, to speak frankly, I do not like my present abode so much as I used to like my old one. Somehow the latter seemed more cosy, dearest. Of course, this room is a good one enough; in fact, in SOME respects it is the more cheerful and interesting of the two. I have nothing to say against it—no. Yet I miss the room that used to be so familiar to me. Old lodgers like myself soon grow as attached to our chattels as to a kinsman. My old room was such a snug little place! True, its walls resembled those of any other room—I am not speaking of that; the point is that the recollection of them seems to haunt my mind with sadness. Curious that recollections should be so mournful! Even what in that room used to vex me and inconvenience me now looms in a purified light, and figures in my imagination as a thing to be desired. We used to live there so quietly—I and an old landlady who is now dead. How my heart aches to remember her, for she was a good woman, and never overcharged for her rooms. Her whole time was spent in making patchwork quilts with knitting-needles that were an arshin [An ell.] long. Oftentimes we shared the same candle and board. Also she had a granddaughter, Masha—a girl who was then a mere baby, but must now be a girl of thirteen. This little piece of mischief, how she used to make us laugh the day long! We lived together, a happy family of three. Often of a long winter's evening we would first have tea at the big round table, and then betake ourselves to our work; the while that, to amuse the child and to keep her out of mischief, the old lady would set herself to tell stories. What stories they were!—though stories less suitable for a child than for a grown-up, educated person. My word! Why, I myself have sat listening to them, as I smoked my pipe, until I have forgotten about work altogether. And then, as the story grew grimmer, the little child, our little bag of mischief, would grow thoughtful in proportion, and clasp her rosy cheeks in her tiny hands, and, hiding her face, press closer to the old landlady. Ah, how I loved to see her at those moments! As one gazed at her one would fail to notice how the candle was flickering, or how the storm was swishing the snow about the courtyard. Yes, that was a goodly life, my Barbara, and we lived it for nearly twenty years.... How my tongue does carry me away! Maybe the subject does not interest you, and I myself find it a not over-easy subject to recall—especially at the present time.

Darkness is falling, and Theresa is busying herself with something or another. My head and my back are aching, and even my thoughts seem to be in pain, so strangely do they occur. Yes, my heart is sad today, Barbara.... What is it you have written to me?—"Why do you not come in PERSON to see me?" Dear one, what would people say? I should have but to cross the courtyard for people to begin noticing us, and asking themselves questions. Gossip and scandal would arise, and there would be read into the affair quite another meaning than the real one. No, little angel, it were better that I should see you tomorrow at Vespers. That will be the better plan, and less hurtful to us both. Nor must you chide me, beloved, because I have written you a letter like this (reading it through, I see it to be all odds and ends); for I am an old man now, dear Barbara, and an uneducated one. Little learning had I in my youth, and things refuse to fix themselves in my brain when I try to learn them anew. No, I am not skilled in letter-writing, Barbara, and, without being told so, or any one laughing at me for it, I know that, whenever I try to describe anything with more than ordinary distinctness, I fall into the mistake of talking sheer rubbish.... I saw you at your window today—yes, I saw you as you were drawing down the blind! Good-bye, goodbye, little Barbara, and may God keep you! Good-bye, my own Barbara Alexievna!—Your sincere friend,

MAKAR DIEVUSHKIN.

P.S.—Do not think that I could write to you in a satirical vein, for I am too old to show my teeth to no purpose, and people would laugh at me, and quote our Russian proverb: "Who diggeth a pit for another one, the same shall fall into it himself."

April 9th

MY DEAREST MAKAR ALEXIEVITCH—Are not you, my friend and benefactor, just a little ashamed to repine and give way to such despondency? And surely you are not offended with me? Ah! Though often thoughtless in my speech, I never should have imagined that you would take my words as a jest at your expense. Rest assured that NEVER should I make sport of your years or of your character. Only my own levity is at fault; still more, the fact that I am so weary of life.

What will such a feeling not engender? To tell you the truth, I had supposed that YOU were jesting in your letter; wherefore, my heart was feeling heavy at the thought that you could feel so displeased with me. Kind comrade and helper, you will be doing me an injustice if for a single moment you ever suspect that I am lacking in feeling or in gratitude towards you. My heart, believe me, is able to appraise at its true worth all that you have done for me by protecting me from my enemies, and from hatred and persecution. Never shall I cease to pray to God for you; and, should my prayers ever reach Him and be received of Heaven, then assuredly fortune will smile upon you!

Today I am not well. By turns I shiver and flush with heat, and Thedora is greatly disturbed about me.... Do not scruple to come and see me, Makar Alexievitch. How can it concern other people what you do? You and I are well enough acquainted with each other, and one's own affairs are one's own affairs. Goodbye, Makar Alexievitch, for I have come to the end of all I had to say, and am feeling too unwell to write more. Again I beg of you not to be angry with me, but to rest assured of my constant respect and attachment.—Your humble, devoted servant,

BARBARA DOBROSELOVA.

April 12th

DEAREST MISTRESS BARBARA ALEXIEVNA—I pray you, my beloved, to tell me what ails you. Every one of your letters fills me with alarm. On the other hand, in every letter I urge you to be more careful of yourself, and to wrap up yourself warmly, and to avoid going out in bad weather, and to be in all things prudent. Yet you go and disobey me! Ah, little angel, you are a perfect child! I know well that you are as weak as a blade of grass, and that, no matter what wind blows upon you, you are ready to fade. But you must be careful of yourself, dearest; you MUST look after yourself better; you MUST avoid all risks, lest you plunge your friends into desolation and despair.

Dearest, you also express a wish to learn the details of my daily life and surroundings. That wish I hasten to satisfy. Let me begin at the beginning, since, by doing so, I shall explain things more systematically. In the first place, on entering this house, one passes into a very bare hall, and thence along a passage to a mean staircase. The reception room, however, is bright, clean, and spacious, and is lined with redwood and metal-work. But the scullery you would not care to see; it is greasy, dirty, and odoriferous, while the stairs are in rags, and the walls so covered with filth that the hand sticks fast wherever it touches them. Also, on each landing there is a medley of boxes, chairs, and dilapidated wardrobes; while the windows have had most of their panes shattered, and everywhere stand washtubs filled with dirt, litter, eggshells, and fish-bladders. The smell is abominable. In short, the house is not a nice one.

As to the disposition of the rooms, I have described it to you already. True, they are convenient enough, yet every one of them has an ATMOSPHERE. I do not mean that they smell badly so much as that each of them seems to contain something which gives forth a rank, sickly-sweet odour. At first the impression is an unpleasant one, but a couple of minutes will suffice to dissipate it, for the reason that EVERYTHING here smells—people's clothes, hands, and everything else—and one grows accustomed to the rankness. Canaries, however, soon die in this house. A naval officer here has just bought his fifth. Birds cannot live long in such an air. Every morning, when fish or beef is being cooked, and washing and scrubbing are in progress, the house is filled with steam. Always, too, the kitchen is full of linen hanging out to dry; and since my room adjoins that apartment, the smell from the clothes causes me not a little annoyance. However, one can grow used to anything.

From earliest dawn the house is astir as its inmates rise, walk about, and stamp their feet. That is to say, everyone who has to go to work then gets out of bed. First of all, tea is partaken of. Most of the tea-urns belong to the landlady; and since there are not very many of them, we have to wait our turn. Anyone who fails to do so will find his teapot emptied and put away. On the first occasion, that was what happened to myself. Well, is there anything else to tell you? Already I have made the acquaintance of the company here. The naval officer took the initiative in calling upon me, and his frankness was such that he told me all about his father, his mother, his sister (who is married to a lawyer of Tula), and the town of Kronstadt. Also, he promised me his patronage, and asked me to come and take tea with him. I kept the appointment in a room where card-playing is continually in progress; and, after tea had been drunk, efforts were made to induce me to gamble. Whether or not my refusal seemed to the company ridiculous I cannot say, but at all events my companions played the whole evening, and were playing when I left. The dust and smoke in the room made my eyes ache. I declined, as I say, to play cards, and was, therefore, requested to discourse on philosophy, after which no one spoke to me at all—a result which I did not regret. In fact, I have no intention of going there again, since every one is for gambling, and for nothing but gambling. Even the literary tchinovnik gives such parties in his room—though, in his case, everything is done delicately and with a certain refinement, so that the thing has something of a retiring and innocent air.

In passing, I may tell you that our landlady is NOT a nice woman. In fact, she is a regular beldame. You have seen her once, so what do you think of her? She is as lanky as a plucked chicken in consumption, and, with Phaldoni (her servant), constitutes the entire staff of the establishment. Whether or not Phaldoni has any other name I do not know, but at least he answers to this one, and every one calls him by it. A red-haired, swine-jowled, snub-nosed, crooked lout, he is for ever wrangling with Theresa, until the pair nearly come to blows. In short, life is not overly pleasant in this place. Never at any time is the household wholly at rest, for always there are people sitting up to play cards. Sometimes, too, certain things are done of which it would be shameful for me to speak. In particular, hardened though I am, it astonishes me that men WITH FAMILIES should care to live in this Sodom. For example, there is a family of poor folk who have rented from the landlady a room which does not adjoin the other rooms, but is set apart in a corner by itself. Yet what quiet people they are! Not a sound is to be heard from them. The father—he is called Gorshkov—is a little grey-headed tchinovnik who, seven years ago, was dismissed from public service, and now walks about in a coat so dirty and ragged that it hurts one to see it. Indeed it is a worse coat even than mine! Also, he is so thin and frail (at times I meet him in the corridor) that his knees quake under him, his hands and head are tremulous with some disease (God only knows what!), and he so fears and distrusts everybody that he always walks alone. Reserved though I myself am, he is even worse. As for his family, it consists of a wife and three children. The eldest of the latter—a boy—is as frail as his father, while the mother—a woman who, formerly, must have been good looking, and still has a striking aspect in spite of her pallor—goes about in the sorriest of rags. Also I have heard that they are in debt to our landlady, as well as that she is not overly kind to them. Moreover, I have heard that Gorshkov lost his post through some unpleasantness or other—through a legal suit or process of which I could not exactly tell you the nature. Yes, they certainly are poor—Oh, my God, how poor! At the same time, never a sound comes from their room. It is as though not a soul were living in it. Never does one hear even the children—which is an unusual thing, seeing that children are ever ready to sport and play, and if they fail to do so it is a bad sign. One evening when I chanced to be passing the door of their room, and all was quiet in the house, I heard through the door a sob, and then a whisper, and then another sob, as though somebody within were weeping, and with such subdued bitterness that it tore my heart to hear the sound. In fact, the thought of these poor people never left me all night, and quite prevented me from sleeping.

Well, good-bye, my little Barbara, my little friend beyond price. I have described to you everything to the best of my ability. All today you have been in my thoughts; all today my heart has been yearning for you. I happen to know, dearest one, that you lack a warm cloak. To me too, these St. Petersburg springs, with their winds and their snow showers, spell death. Good heavens, how the breezes bite one! Do not be angry, beloved, that I should write like this. Style I have not. Would that I had! I write just what wanders into my brain, in the hope that I may cheer you up a little. Of course, had I had a good education, things might have been different; but, as things were, I could not have one. Never did I learn even to do simple sums!—Your faithful and unchangeable friend,

MAKAR DIEVUSHKIN.

April 25th

MY DEAREST MAKAR ALEXIEVITCH—Today I met my cousin Sasha. To see her going to wrack and ruin shocked me terribly. Moreover, it has reached me, through a side wind, that she has been making inquiry for me, and dogging my footsteps, under the pretext that she wishes to pardon me, to forget the past, and to renew our acquaintance. Well, among other things she told me that, whereas you are not a kinsman of mine, that she is my nearest relative; that you have no right whatever to enter into family relations with us; and that it is wrong and shameful for me to be living upon your earnings and charity. Also, she said that I must have forgotten all that she did for me, though thereby she saved both myself and my mother from starvation, and gave us food and drink; that for two and a half years we caused her great loss; and, above all things, that she excused us what we owed her. Even my poor mother she did not spare. Would that she, my dead parent, could know how I am being treated! But God knows all about it.... Also, Anna declared that it was solely through my own fault that my fortunes declined after she had bettered them; that she is in no way responsible for what then happened; and that I have but myself to blame for having been either unable or unwilling to defend my honour. Great God! WHO, then, has been at fault? According to Anna, Hospodin [Mr.] Bwikov was only right when he declined to marry a woman who—But need I say it? It is cruel to hear such lies as hers. What is to become of me I do not know. I tremble and sob and weep. Indeed, even to write this letter has cost me two hours. At least it might have been thought that Anna would have confessed HER share in the past. Yet see what she says!... For the love of God do not be anxious about me, my friend, my only benefactor. Thedora is over apt to exaggerate matters. I am not REALLY ill. I have merely caught a little cold. I caught it last night while I was walking to Bolkovo, to hear Mass sung for my mother. Ah, mother, my poor mother! Could you but rise from the grave and learn what is being done to your daughter!

B. D.

May 20th

MY DEAREST LITTLE BARBARA—I am sending you a few grapes, which are good for a convalescent person, and strongly recommended by doctors for the allayment of fever. Also, you were saying the other day that you would like some roses; wherefore, I now send you a bunch. Are you at all able to eat, my darling?—for that is the chief point which ought to be seen to. Let us thank God that the past and all its unhappiness are gone! Yes, let us give thanks to Heaven for that much! As for books, I cannot get hold of any, except for a book which, written in excellent style, is, I believe, to be had here. At all events, people keep praising it very much, and I have begged the loan of it for myself. Should you too like to read it? In this respect, indeed, I feel nervous, for the reason that it is so difficult to divine what your taste in books may be, despite my knowledge of your character. Probably you would like poetry—the poetry of sentiment and of love making? Well, I will send you a book of MY OWN poems. Already I have copied out part of the manuscript.

Everything with me is going well; so pray do not be anxious on my account, beloved. What Thedora told you about me was sheer rubbish. Tell her from me that she has not been speaking the truth. Yes, do not fail to give this mischief-maker my message. It is not the case that I have gone and sold a new uniform. Why should I do so, seeing that I have forty roubles of salary still to come to me? Do not be uneasy, my darling. Thedora is a vindictive woman—merely a vindictive woman. We shall yet see better days. Only do you get well, my angel—only do you get well, for the love of God, lest you grieve an old man. Also, who told you that I was looking thin? Slanders again—nothing but slanders! I am as healthy as could be, and have grown so fat that I am ashamed to be so sleek of paunch. Would that you were equally healthy!... Now goodbye, my angel. I kiss every one of your tiny fingers, and remain ever your constant friend,

MAKAR DIEVUSHKIN.

P.S.—But what is this, dearest one, that you have written to me? Why do you place me upon such a pedestal? Moreover, how could I come and visit you frequently? How, I repeat? Of course, I might avail myself of the cover of night; but, alas! the season of the year is what it is, and includes no night time to speak of. In fact, although, throughout your illness and delirium, I scarcely left your side for a moment, I cannot think how I contrived to do the many things that I did. Later, I ceased to visit you at all, for the reason that people were beginning to notice things, and to ask me questions. Yet, even so, a scandal has arisen. Theresa I trust thoroughly, for she is not a talkative woman; but consider how it will be when the truth comes out in its entirety! What THEN will folk not say and think? Nevertheless, be of good cheer, my beloved, and regain your health. When you have done so we will contrive to arrange a rendezvous out of doors.

June 1st

MY BELOVED MAKAR ALEXIEVITCH—So eager am I to do something that will please and divert you in return for your care, for your ceaseless efforts on my behalf—in short, for your love for me—that I have decided to beguile a leisure hour for you by delving into my locker, and extracting thence the manuscript which I send you herewith. I began it during the happier period of my life, and have continued it at intervals since. So often have you asked me about my former existence—about my mother, about Pokrovski, about my sojourn with Anna Thedorovna, about my more recent misfortunes; so often have you expressed an earnest desire to read the manuscript in which (God knows why) I have recorded certain incidents of my life, that I feel no doubt but that the sending of it will give you sincere pleasure. Yet somehow I feel depressed when I read it, for I seem now to have grown twice as old as I was when I penned its concluding lines. Ah, Makar Alexievitch, how weary I am—how this insomnia tortures me! Convalescence is indeed a hard thing to bear!

B. D.

I

UP to the age of fourteen, when my father died, my childhood was the happiest period of my life. It began very far away from here in the depths of the province of Tula, where my father filled the position of steward on the vast estates of the Prince P—. Our house was situated in one of the Prince's villages, and we lived a quiet, obscure, but happy, life. A gay little child was I—my one idea being ceaselessly to run about the fields and the woods and the garden. No one ever gave me a thought, for my father was always occupied with business affairs, and my mother with her housekeeping. Nor did any one ever give me any lessons—a circumstance for which I was not sorry. At earliest dawn I would hie me to a pond or a copse, or to a hay or a harvest field, where the sun could warm me, and I could roam wherever I liked, and scratch my hands with bushes, and tear my clothes in pieces. For this I used to get blamed afterwards, but I did not care.

Had it befallen me never to quit that village—had it befallen me to remain for ever in that spot—I should always have been happy; but fate ordained that I should leave my birthplace even before my girlhood had come to an end. In short, I was only twelve years old when we removed to St. Petersburg. Ah! how it hurts me to recall the mournful gatherings before our departure, and to recall how bitterly I wept when the time came for us to say farewell to all that I had held so dear! I remember throwing myself upon my father's neck, and beseeching him with tears to stay in the country a little longer; but he bid me be silent, and my mother, adding her tears to mine, explained that business matters compelled us to go. As a matter of fact, old Prince P— had just died, and his heirs had dismissed my father from his post; whereupon, since he had a little money privately invested in St. Petersburg, he bethought him that his personal presence in the capital was necessary for the due management of his affairs. It was my mother who told me this. Consequently we settled here in St. Petersburg, and did not again move until my father died.

How difficult I found it to grow accustomed to my new life! At the time of our removal to St. Petersburg it was autumn—a season when, in the country, the weather is clear and keen and bright, all agricultural labour has come to an end, the great sheaves of corn are safely garnered in the byre, and the birds are flying hither and thither in clamorous flocks. Yes, at that season the country is joyous and fair, but here in St. Petersburg, at the time when we reached the city, we encountered nothing but rain, bitter autumn frosts, dull skies, ugliness, and crowds of strangers who looked hostile, discontented, and disposed to take offence. However, we managed to settle down—though I remember that in our new home there was much noise and confusion as we set the establishment in order. After this my father was seldom at home, and my mother had few spare moments; wherefore, I found myself forgotten.

The first morning after our arrival, when I awoke from sleep, how sad I felt! I could see that our windows looked out upon a drab space of wall, and that the street below was littered with filth. Passers-by were few, and as they walked they kept muffling themselves up against the cold.

Then there ensued days when dullness and depression reigned supreme. Scarcely a relative or an acquaintance did we possess in St. Petersburg, and even Anna Thedorovna and my father had come to loggerheads with one another, owing to the fact that he owed her money. In fact, our only visitors were business callers, and as a rule these came but to wrangle, to argue, and to raise a disturbance. Such visits would make my father look very discontented, and seem out of temper. For hours and hours he would pace the room with a frown on his face and a brooding silence on his lips. Even my mother did not dare address him at these times, while, for my own part, I used to sit reading quietly and humbly in a corner—not venturing to make a movement of any sort.

Three months after our arrival in St. Petersburg I was sent to a boarding-school. Here I found myself thrown among strange people; here everything was grim and uninviting, with teachers continually shouting at me, and my fellow-pupils for ever holding me up to derision, and myself constantly feeling awkward and uncouth. How strict, how exacting was the system! Appointed hours for everything, a common table, ever-insistent teachers! These things simply worried and tortured me. Never from the first could I sleep, but used to weep many a chill, weary night away. In the evenings everyone would have to repeat or to learn her lessons. As I crouched over a dialogue or a vocabulary, without daring even to stir, how my thoughts would turn to the chimney-corner at home, to my father, to my mother, to my old nurse, to the tales which the latter had been used to tell! How sad it all was! The memory of the merest trifle at home would please me, and I would think and think how nice things used to be at home. Once more I would be sitting in our little parlour at tea with my parents—in the familiar little parlour where everything was snug and warm! How ardently, how convulsively I would seem to be embracing my mother! Thus I would ponder, until at length tears of sorrow would softly gush forth and choke my bosom, and drive the lessons out of my head. For I never could master the tasks of the morrow; no matter how much my mistress and fellow-pupils might gird at me, no matter how much I might repeat my lessons over and over to myself, knowledge never came with the morning. Consequently, I used to be ordered the kneeling punishment, and given only one meal in the day. How dull and dispirited I used to feel! From the first my fellow-pupils used to tease and deride and mock me whenever I was saying my lessons. Also, they used to pinch me as we were on our way to dinner or tea, and to make groundless complaints of me to the head mistress. On the other hand, how heavenly it seemed when, on Saturday evening, my old nurse arrived to fetch me! How I would embrace the old woman in transports of joy! After dressing me, and wrapping me up, she would find that she could scarcely keep pace with me on the way home, so full was I of chatter and tales about one thing and another. Then, when I had arrived home merry and lighthearted, how fervently I would embrace my parents, as though I had not seen them for ten years. Such a fussing would there be—such a talking and a telling of tales! To everyone I would run with a greeting, and laugh, and giggle, and scamper about, and skip for very joy. True, my father and I used to have grave conversations about lessons and teachers and the French language and grammar; yet we were all very happy and contented together. Even now it thrills me to think of those moments. For my father's sake I tried hard to learn my lessons, for I could see that he was spending his last kopeck upon me, and himself subsisting God knows how. Every day he grew more morose and discontented and irritable; every day his character kept changing for the worse. He had suffered an influx of debts, nor were his business affairs prospering. As for my mother, she was afraid even to say a word, or to weep aloud, for fear of still further angering him. Gradually she sickened, grew thinner and thinner, and became taken with a painful cough. Whenever I reached home from school I would find every one low-spirited, and my mother shedding silent tears, and my father raging. Bickering and high words would arise, during which my father was wont to declare that, though he no longer derived the smallest pleasure or relaxation from life, and had spent his last coin upon my education, I had not yet mastered the French language. In short, everything began to go wrong, to turn to unhappiness; and for that circumstance, my father took vengeance upon myself and my mother. How he could treat my poor mother so I cannot understand. It used to rend my heart to see her, so hollow were her cheeks becoming, so sunken her eyes, so hectic her face. But it was chiefly around myself that the disputes raged. Though beginning only with some trifle, they would soon go on to God knows what. Frequently, even I myself did not know to what they related. Anything and everything would enter into them, for my father would say that I was an utter dunce at the French language; that the head mistress of my school was a stupid, common sort of women who cared nothing for morals; that he (my father) had not yet succeeded in obtaining another post; that Lamonde's "Grammar" was a wretched book— even a worse one than Zapolski's; that a great deal of money had been squandered upon me; that it was clear that I was wasting my time in repeating dialogues and vocabularies; that I alone was at fault, and that I must answer for everything. Yet this did not arise from any WANT OF LOVE for me on the part of my father, but rather from the fact that he was incapable of putting himself in my own and my mother's place. It came of a defect of character.

All these cares and worries and disappointments tortured my poor father until he became moody and distrustful. Next he began to neglect his health, with the result that, catching a chill, he died, after a short illness, so suddenly and unexpectedly that for a few days we were almost beside ourselves with the shock—my mother, in particular, lying for a while in such a state of torpor that I had fears for her reason. The instant my father was dead creditors seemed to spring up out of the ground, and to assail us en masse. Everything that we possessed had to be surrendered to them, including a little house which my father had bought six months after our arrival in St. Petersburg. How matters were finally settled I do not know, but we found ourselves roofless, shelterless, and without a copper. My mother was grievously ill, and of means of subsistence we had none. Before us there loomed only ruin, sheer ruin. At the time I was fourteen years old. Soon afterwards Anna Thedorovna came to see us, saying that she was a lady of property and our relative; and this my mother confirmed—though, true, she added that Anna was only a very DISTANT relative. Anna had never taken the least notice of us during my father's lifetime, yet now she entered our presence with tears in her eyes, and an assurance that she meant to better our fortunes. Having condoled with us on our loss and destitute position, she added that my father had been to blame for everything, in that he had lived beyond his means, and taken upon himself more than he was able to perform. Also, she expressed a wish to draw closer to us, and to forget old scores; and when my mother explained that, for her own part, she harboured no resentment against Anna, the latter burst into tears, and, hurrying my mother away to church, then and there ordered Mass to be said for the "dear departed," as she called my father. In this manner she effected a solemn reconciliation with my mother.

Next, after long negotiations and vacillations, coupled with much vivid description of our destitute position, our desolation, and our helplessness, Anna invited us to pay her (as she expressed it) a "return visit." For this my mother duly thanked her, and considered the invitation for a while; after which, seeing that there was nothing else to be done, she informed Anna Thedorovna that she was prepared, gratefully, to accept her offer. Ah, how I remember the morning when we removed to Vassilievski Island! [A quarter of St. Petersburg.] It was a clear, dry, frosty morning in autumn. My mother could not restrain her tears, and I too felt depressed. Nay, my very heart seemed to be breaking under a strange, undefined load of sorrow. How terrible it all seemed!...

II

AT first—that is to say, until my mother and myself grew used to our new abode—we found living at Anna Thedorovna's both strange and disagreeable. The house was her own, and contained five rooms, three of which she shared with my orphaned cousin, Sasha (whom she had brought up from babyhood); a fourth was occupied by my mother and myself; and the fifth was rented of Anna by a poor student named Pokrovski. Although Anna lived in good style—in far better style than might have been expected—her means and her avocation were conjectural. Never was she at rest; never was she not busy with some mysterious something or other. Also, she possessed a wide and varied circle of friends. The stream of callers was perpetual—although God only knows who they were, or what their business was. No sooner did my mother hear the door-bell ring than off she would carry me to our own apartment. This greatly displeased Anna, who used again and again to assure my mother that we were too proud for our station in life. In fact, she would sulk for hours about it. At the time I could not understand these reproaches, and it was not until long afterwards that I learned—or rather, I guessed—why eventually my mother declared that she could not go on living with Anna. Yes, Anna was a bad woman. Never did she let us alone. As to the exact motive why she had asked us to come and share her house with her I am still in the dark. At first she was not altogether unkind to us but, later, she revealed to us her real character—as soon, that is to say, as she saw that we were at her mercy, and had nowhere else to go. Yes, in early days she was quite kind to me—even offensively so, but afterwards, I had to suffer as much as my mother. Constantly did Anna reproach us; constantly did she remind us of her benefactions, and introduce us to her friends as poor relatives of hers whom, out of goodness of heart and for the love of Christ, she had received into her bosom. At table, also, she would watch every mouthful that we took; and, if our appetite failed, immediately she would begin as before, and reiterate that we were over-dainty, that we must not assume that riches would mean happiness, and that we had better go and live by ourselves. Moreover, she never ceased to inveigh against my father—saying that he had sought to be better than other people, and thereby had brought himself to a bad end; that he had left his wife and daughter destitute; and that, but for the fact that we had happened to meet with a kind and sympathetic Christian soul, God alone knew where we should have laid our heads, save in the street. What did that woman not say? To hear her was not so much galling as disgusting. From time to time my mother would burst into tears, her health grew worse from day to day, and her body was becoming sheer skin and bone. All the while, too, we had to work—to work from morning till night, for we had contrived to obtain some employment as occasional sempstresses. This, however, did not please Anna, who used to tell us that there was no room in her house for a modiste's establishment. Yet we had to get clothes to wear, to provide for unforeseen expenses, and to have a little money at our disposal in case we should some day wish to remove elsewhere. Unfortunately, the strain undermined my mother's health, and she became gradually weaker. Sickness, like a cankerworm, was gnawing at her life, and dragging her towards the tomb. Well could I see what she was enduring, what she was suffering. Yes, it all lay open to my eyes.

Day succeeded day, and each day was like the last one. We lived a life as quiet as though we had been in the country. Anna herself grew quieter in proportion as she came to realise the extent of her power over us. In nothing did we dare to thwart her. From her portion of the house our apartment was divided by a corridor, while next to us (as mentioned above) dwelt a certain Pokrovski, who was engaged in teaching Sasha the French and German languages, as well as history and geography—"all the sciences," as Anna used to say. In return for these services he received free board and lodging. As for Sasha, she was a clever, but rude and uncouth, girl of thirteen. On one occasion Anna remarked to my mother that it might be as well if I also were to take some lessons, seeing that my education had been neglected at school; and, my mother joyfully assenting, I joined Sasha for a year in studying under this Pokrovski.

The latter was a poor—a very poor—young man whose health would not permit of his undertaking the regular university course. Indeed, it was only for form's sake that we called him "The Student." He lived in such a quiet, humble, retiring fashion that never a sound reached us from his room. Also, his exterior was peculiar—he moved and walked awkwardly, and uttered his words in such a strange manner that at first I could never look at him without laughing. Sasha was for ever playing tricks upon him—more especially when he was giving us our lessons. But unfortunately, he was of a temperament as excitable as herself. Indeed, he was so irritable that the least trifle would send him into a frenzy, and set him shouting at us, and complaining of our conduct. Sometimes he would even rush away to his room before school hours were over, and sit there for days over his books, of which he had a store that was both rare and valuable. In addition, he acted as teacher at another establishment, and received payment for his services there; and, whenever he had received his fees for this extra work, he would hasten off and purchase more books.

In time I got to know and like him better, for in reality he was a good, worthy fellow—more so than any of the people with whom we otherwise came in contact. My mother in particular had a great respect for him, and, after herself, he was my best friend. But at first I was just an overgrown hoyden, and joined Sasha in playing the fool. For hours we would devise tricks to anger and distract him, for he looked extremely ridiculous when he was angry, and so diverted us the more (ashamed though I am now to admit it). But once, when we had driven him nearly to tears, I heard him say to himself under his breath, "What cruel children!" and instantly I repented—I began to feel sad and ashamed and sorry for him. I reddened to my ears, and begged him, almost with tears, not to mind us, nor to take offence at our stupid jests. Nevertheless, without finishing the lesson, he closed his book, and departed to his own room. All that day I felt torn with remorse. To think that we two children had forced him, the poor, the unhappy one, to remember his hard lot! And at night I could not sleep for grief and regret. Remorse is said to bring relief to the soul, but it is not so. How far my grief was internally connected with my conceit I do not know, but at least I did not wish him to think me a baby, seeing that I had now reached the age of fifteen years. Therefore, from that day onwards I began to torture my imagination with devising a thousand schemes which should compel Pokrovski to alter his opinion of me. At the same time, being yet shy and reserved by nature, I ended by finding that, in my present position, I could make up my mind to nothing but vague dreams (and such dreams I had). However, I ceased to join Sasha in playing the fool, while Pokrovski, for his part, ceased to lose his temper with us so much. Unfortunately this was not enough to satisfy my self-esteem.

At this point, I must say a few words about the strangest, the most interesting, the most pitiable human being that I have ever come across. I speak of him now—at this particular point in these memoirs—for the reason that hitherto I had paid him no attention whatever, and began to do so now only because everything connected with Pokrovski had suddenly become of absorbing interest in my eyes.

Sometimes there came to the house a ragged, poorly-dressed, grey-headed, awkward, amorphous—in short, a very strange-looking—little old man. At first glance it might have been thought that he was perpetually ashamed of something—that he had on his conscience something which always made him, as it were, bristle up and then shrink into himself. Such curious starts and grimaces did he indulge in that one was forced to conclude that he was scarcely in his right mind. On arriving, he would halt for a while by the window in the hall, as though afraid to enter; until, should any one happen to pass in or out of the door—whether Sasha or myself or one of the servants (to the latter he always resorted the most readily, as being the most nearly akin to his own class)—he would begin to gesticulate and to beckon to that person, and to make various signs. Then, should the person in question nod to him, or call him by name (the recognised token that no other visitor was present, and that he might enter freely), he would open the door gently, give a smile of satisfaction as he rubbed his hands together, and proceed on tiptoe to young Pokrovski's room. This old fellow was none other than Pokrovski's father.

Later I came to know his story in detail. Formerly a civil servant, he had possessed no additional means, and so had occupied a very low and insignificant position in the service. Then, after his first wife (mother of the younger Pokrovski) had died, the widower bethought him of marrying a second time, and took to himself a tradesman's daughter, who soon assumed the reins over everything, and brought the home to rack and ruin, so that the old man was worse off than before. But to the younger Pokrovski, fate proved kinder, for a landowner named Bwikov, who had formerly known the lad's father and been his benefactor, took the boy under his protection, and sent him to school. Another reason why this Bwikov took an interest in young Pokrovski was that he had known the lad's dead mother, who, while still a serving-maid, had been befriended by Anna Thedorovna, and subsequently married to the elder Pokrovski. At the wedding Bwikov, actuated by his friendship for Anna, conferred upon the young bride a dowry of five thousand roubles; but whither that money had since disappeared I cannot say. It was from Anna's lips that I heard the story, for the student Pokrovski was never prone to talk about his family affairs. His mother was said to have been very good-looking; wherefore, it is the more mysterious why she should have made so poor a match. She died when young—only four years after her espousal.

From school the young Pokrovski advanced to a gymnasium, [Secondary school.] and thence to the University, where Bwikov, who frequently visited the capital, continued to accord the youth his protection. Gradually, however, ill health put an end to the young man's university course; whereupon Bwikov introduced and personally recommended him to Anna Thedorovna, and he came to lodge with her on condition that he taught Sasha whatever might be required of him.

Grief at the harshness of his wife led the elder Pokrovski to plunge into dissipation, and to remain in an almost permanent condition of drunkenness. Constantly his wife beat him, or sent him to sit in the kitchen—with the result that in time, he became so inured to blows and neglect, that he ceased to complain. Still not greatly advanced in years, he had nevertheless endangered his reason through evil courses—his only sign of decent human feeling being his love for his son. The latter was said to resemble his dead mother as one pea may resemble another. What recollections, therefore, of the kind helpmeet of former days may not have moved the breast of the poor broken old man to this boundless affection for the boy? Of naught else could the father ever speak but of his son, and never did he fail to visit him twice a week. To come oftener he did not dare, for the reason that the younger Pokrovski did not like these visits of his father's. In fact, there can be no doubt that the youth's greatest fault was his lack of filial respect. Yet the father was certainly rather a difficult person to deal with, for, in the first place, he was extremely inquisitive, while, in the second place, his long-winded conversation and questions—questions of the most vapid and senseless order conceivable—always prevented the son from working. Likewise, the old man occasionally arrived there drunk. Gradually, however, the son was weaning his parent from his vicious ways and everlasting inquisitiveness, and teaching the old man to look upon him, his son, as an oracle, and never to speak without that son's permission.

On the subject of his Petinka, as he called him, the poor old man could never sufficiently rhapsodise and dilate. Yet when he arrived to see his son he almost invariably had on his face a downcast, timid expression that was probably due to uncertainty concerning the way in which he would be received. For a long time he would hesitate to enter, and if I happened to be there he would question me for twenty minutes or so as to whether his Petinka was in good health, as well as to the sort of mood he was in, whether he was engaged on matters of importance, what precisely he was doing (writing or meditating), and so on. Then, when I had sufficiently encouraged and reassured the old man, he would make up his mind to enter, and quietly and cautiously open the door. Next, he would protrude his head through the chink, and if he saw that his son was not angry, but threw him a nod, he would glide noiselessly into the room, take off his scarf, and hang up his hat (the latter perennially in a bad state of repair, full of holes, and with a smashed brim)—the whole being done without a word or a sound of any kind. Next, the old man would seat himself warily on a chair, and, never removing his eyes from his son, follow his every movement, as though seeking to gauge Petinka's state of mind. On the other hand, if the son was not in good spirits, the father would make a note of the fact, and at once get up, saying that he had "only called for a minute or two," that, "having been out for a long walk, and happening at the moment to be passing," he had "looked in for a moment's rest." Then silently and humbly the old man would resume his hat and scarf; softly he would open the door, and noiselessly depart with a forced smile on his face— the better to bear the disappointment which was seething in his breast, the better to help him not to show it to his son.

On the other hand, whenever the son received his father civilly the old man would be struck dumb with joy. Satisfaction would beam in his face, in his every gesture, in his every movement. And if the son deigned to engage in conversation with him, the old man always rose a little from his chair, and answered softly, sympathetically, with something like reverence, while strenuously endeavouring to make use of the most recherche (that is to say, the most ridiculous) expressions. But, alas! He had not the gift of words. Always he grew confused, and turned red in the face; never did he know what to do with his hands or with himself. Likewise, whenever he had returned an answer of any kind, he would go on repeating the same in a whisper, as though he were seeking to justify what he had just said. And if he happened to have returned a good answer, he would begin to preen himself, and to straighten his waistcoat, frockcoat and tie, and to assume an air of conscious dignity. Indeed, on these occasions he would feel so encouraged, he would carry his daring to such a pitch, that, rising softly from his chair, he would approach the bookshelves, take thence a book, and read over to himself some passage or another. All this he would do with an air of feigned indifference and sangfroid, as though he were free ALWAYS to use his son's books, and his son's kindness were no rarity at all. Yet on one occasion I saw the poor old fellow actually turn pale on being told by his son not to touch the books. Abashed and confused, he, in his awkward hurry, replaced the volume wrong side uppermost; whereupon, with a supreme effort to recover himself, he turned it round with a smile and a blush, as though he were at a loss how to view his own misdemeanour. Gradually, as already said, the younger Pokrovski weaned his father from his dissipated ways by giving him a small coin whenever, on three successive occasions, he (the father) arrived sober. Sometimes, also, the younger man would buy the older one shoes, or a tie, or a waistcoat; whereafter, the old man would be as proud of his acquisition as a peacock. Not infrequently, also, the old man would step in to visit ourselves, and bring Sasha and myself gingerbread birds or apples, while talking unceasingly of Petinka. Always he would beg of us to pay attention to our lessons, on the plea that Petinka was a good son, an exemplary son, a son who was in twofold measure a man of learning; after which he would wink at us so quizzingly with his left eye, and twist himself about in such amusing fashion, that we were forced to burst out laughing. My mother had a great liking for him, but he detested Anna Thedorovna—although in her presence he would be quieter than water and lowlier than the earth.

Soon after this I ceased to take lessons of Pokrovski. Even now he thought me a child, a raw schoolgirl, as much as he did Sasha; and this hurt me extremely, seeing that I had done so much to expiate my former behaviour. Of my efforts in this direction no notice had been taken, and the fact continued to anger me more and more. Scarcely ever did I address a word to my tutor between school hours, for I simply could not bring myself to do it. If I made the attempt I only grew red and confused, and rushed away to weep in a corner. How it would all have ended I do not know, had not a curious incident helped to bring about a rapprochement. One evening, when my mother was sitting in Anna Thedorovna's room, I crept on tiptoe to Pokrovski's apartment, in the belief that he was not at home. Some strange impulse moved me to do so. True, we had lived cheek by jowl with one another; yet never once had I caught a glimpse of his abode. Consequently my heart beat loudly—so loudly, indeed, that it seemed almost to be bursting from my breast. On entering the room I glanced around me with tense interest. The apartment was very poorly furnished, and bore few traces of orderliness. On table and chairs there lay heaps of books; everywhere were books and papers. Then a strange thought entered my head, as well as, with the thought, an unpleasant feeling of irritation. It seemed to me that my friendship, my heart's affection, meant little to him, for HE was well-educated, whereas I was stupid, and had learned nothing, and had read not a single book. So I stood looking wistfully at the long bookshelves where they groaned under their weight of volumes. I felt filled with grief, disappointment, and a sort of frenzy. I felt that I MUST read those books, and decided to do so—to read them one by one, and with all possible speed. Probably the idea was that, by learning whatsoever HE knew, I should render myself more worthy of his friendship. So, I made a rush towards the bookcase nearest me, and, without stopping further to consider matters, seized hold of the first dusty tome upon which my hands chanced to alight, and, reddening and growing pale by turns, and trembling with fear and excitement, clasped the stolen book to my breast with the intention of reading it by candle light while my mother lay asleep at night.

But how vexed I felt when, on returning to our own room, and hastily turning the pages, only an old, battered worm-eaten Latin work greeted my eyes! Without loss of time I retraced my steps. Just when I was about to replace the book I heard a noise in the corridor outside, and the sound of footsteps approaching. Fumblingly I hastened to complete what I was about, but the tiresome book had become so tightly wedged into its row that, on being pulled out, it caused its fellows to close up too compactly to leave any place for their comrade. To insert the book was beyond my strength; yet still I kept pushing and pushing at the row. At last the rusty nail which supported the shelf (the thing seemed to have been waiting on purpose for that moment!) broke off short; with the result that the shelf descended with a crash, and the books piled themselves in a heap on the floor! Then the door of the room opened, and Pokrovski entered!

I must here remark that he never could bear to have his possessions tampered with. Woe to the person, in particular, who touched his books! Judge, therefore, of my horror when books small and great, books of every possible shape and size and thickness, came tumbling from the shelf, and flew and sprang over the table, and under the chairs, and about the whole room. I would have turned and fled, but it was too late. "All is over!" thought I. "All is over! I am ruined, I am undone! Here have I been playing the fool like a ten-year-old child! What a stupid girl I am! The monstrous fool!"

Indeed, Pokrovski was very angry. "What? Have you not done enough?" he cried. "Are you not ashamed to be for ever indulging in such pranks? Are you NEVER going to grow sensible?" With that he darted forward to pick up the books, while I bent down to help him.

"You need not, you need not!" he went on. "You would have done far better not to have entered without an invitation."

Next, a little mollified by my humble demeanour, he resumed in his usual tutorial tone—the tone which he had adopted in his new-found role of preceptor:

"When are you going to grow steadier and more thoughtful? Consider yourself for a moment. You are no longer a child, a little girl, but a maiden of fifteen."

Then, with a desire (probably) to satisfy himself that I was no longer a being of tender years, he threw me a glance—but straightway reddened to his very ears. This I could not understand, but stood gazing at him in astonishment. Presently, he straightened himself a little, approached me with a sort of confused expression, and haltingly said something—probably it was an apology for not having before perceived that I was now a grown-up young person. But the next moment I understood. What I did I hardly know, save that, in my dismay and confusion, I blushed even more hotly than he had done and, covering my face with my hands, rushed from the room.

What to do with myself for shame I could not think. The one thought in my head was that he had surprised me in his room. For three whole days I found myself unable to raise my eyes to his, but blushed always to the point of weeping. The strangest and most confused of thoughts kept entering my brain. One of them—the most extravagant—was that I should dearly like to go to Pokrovski, and to explain to him the situation, and to make full confession, and to tell him everything without concealment, and to assure him that I had not acted foolishly as a minx, but honestly and of set purpose. In fact, I DID make up my mind to take this course, but lacked the necessary courage to do it. If I had done so, what a figure I should have cut! Even now I am ashamed to think of it.

A few days later, my mother suddenly fell dangerously ill. For two days past she had not left her bed, while during the third night of her illness she became seized with fever and delirium. I also had not closed my eyes during the previous night, but now waited upon my mother, sat by her bed, brought her drink at intervals, and gave her medicine at duly appointed hours. The next night I suffered terribly. Every now and then sleep would cause me to nod, and objects grow dim before my eyes. Also, my head was turning dizzy, and I could have fainted for very weariness. Yet always my mother's feeble moans recalled me to myself as I started, momentarily awoke, and then again felt drowsiness overcoming me. What torture it was! I do not know, I cannot clearly remember, but I think that, during a moment when wakefulness was thus contending with slumber, a strange dream, a horrible vision, visited my overwrought brain, and I awoke in terror. The room was nearly in darkness, for the candle was flickering, and throwing stray beams of light which suddenly illuminated the room, danced for a moment on the walls, and then disappeared. Somehow I felt afraid—a sort of horror had come upon me—my imagination had been over-excited by the evil dream which I had experienced, and a feeling of oppression was crushing my heart.... I leapt from the chair, and involuntarily uttered a cry—a cry wrung from me by the terrible, torturing sensation that was upon me. Presently the door opened, and Pokrovski entered.

I remember that I was in his arms when I recovered my senses. Carefully seating me on a bench, he handed me a glass of water, and then asked me a few questions—though how I answered them I do not know. "You yourself are ill," he said as he took my hand. "You yourself are VERY ill. You are feverish, and I can see that you are knocking yourself out through your neglect of your own health. Take a little rest. Lie down and go to sleep. Yes, lie down, lie down," he continued without giving me time to protest. Indeed, fatigue had so exhausted my strength that my eyes were closing from very weakness. So I lay down on the bench with the intention of sleeping for half an hour only; but, I slept till morning. Pokrovski then awoke me, saying that it was time for me to go and give my mother her medicine.

When the next evening, about eight o'clock, I had rested a little and was preparing to spend the night in a chair beside my mother (fixedly meaning not to go to sleep this time), Pokrovski suddenly knocked at the door. I opened it, and he informed me that, since, possibly, I might find the time wearisome, he had brought me a few books to read. I accepted the books, but do not, even now, know what books they were, nor whether I looked into them, despite the fact that I never closed my eyes the whole night long. The truth was that a strange feeling of excitement was preventing me from sleeping, and I could not rest long in any one spot, but had to keep rising from my chair, and walking about the room. Throughout my whole being there seemed to be diffused a kind of elation—of elation at Pokrovski's attentions, at the thought that he was anxious and uneasy about me. Until dawn I pondered and dreamed; and though I felt sure Pokrovski would not again visit us that night, I gave myself up to fancies concerning what he might do the following evening.

That evening, when everyone else in the house had retired to rest, Pokrovski opened his door, and opened a conversation from the threshold of his room. Although, at this distance of time, I cannot remember a word of what we said to one another, I remember that I blushed, grew confused, felt vexed with myself, and awaited with impatience the end of the conversation although I myself had been longing for the meeting to take place, and had spent the day in dreaming of it, and devising a string of suitable questions and replies. Yes, that evening saw the first strand in our friendship knitted; and each subsequent night of my mother's illness we spent several hours together. Little by little I overcame his reserve, but found that each of these conversations left me filled with a sense of vexation at myself. At the same time, I could see with secret joy and a sense of proud elation that I was leading him to forget his tiresome books. At last the conversation turned jestingly upon the upsetting of the shelf. The moment was a peculiar one, for it came upon me just when I was in the right mood for self-revelation and candour. In my ardour, my curious phase of exaltation, I found myself led to make a full confession of the fact that I had become wishful to learn, to KNOW, something, since I had felt hurt at being taken for a chit, a mere baby.... I repeat that that night I was in a very strange frame of mind. My heart was inclined to be tender, and there were tears standing in my eyes. Nothing did I conceal as I told him about my friendship for him, about my desire to love him, about my scheme for living in sympathy with him and comforting him, and making his life easier. In return he threw me a look of confusion mingled with astonishment, and said nothing. Then suddenly I began to feel terribly pained and disappointed, for I conceived that he had failed to understand me, or even that he might be laughing at me. Bursting into tears like a child, I sobbed, and could not stop myself, for I had fallen into a kind of fit; whereupon he seized my hand, kissed it, and clasped it to his breast—saying various things, meanwhile, to comfort me, for he was labouring under a strong emotion. Exactly what he said I do not remember—I merely wept and laughed by turns, and blushed, and found myself unable to speak a word for joy. Yet, for all my agitation, I noticed that about him there still lingered an air of constraint and uneasiness. Evidently, he was lost in wonder at my enthusiasm and raptures—at my curiously ardent, unexpected, consuming friendship. It may be that at first he was amazed, but that afterwards he accepted my devotion and words of invitation and expressions of interest with the same simple frankness as I had offered them, and responded to them with an interest, a friendliness, a devotion equal to my own, even as a friend or a brother would do. How happy, how warm was the feeling in my heart! Nothing had I concealed or repressed. No, I had bared all to his sight, and each day would see him draw nearer to me.

Truly I could not say what we did not talk about during those painful, yet rapturous, hours when, by the trembling light of a lamp, and almost at the very bedside of my poor sick mother, we kept midnight tryst. Whatsoever first came into our heads we spoke of—whatsoever came riven from our hearts, whatsoever seemed to call for utterance, found voice. And almost always we were happy. What a grievous, yet joyous, period it was—a period grievous and joyous at the same time! To this day it both hurts and delights me to recall it. Joyous or bitter though it was, its memories are yet painful. At least they seem so to me, though a certain sweetness assuaged the pain. So, whenever I am feeling heartsick and oppressed and jaded and sad those memories return to freshen and revive me, even as drops of evening dew return to freshen and revive, after a sultry day, the poor faded flower which has long been drooping in the noontide heat.

My mother grew better, but still I continued to spend the nights on a chair by her bedside. Often, too, Pokrovski would give me books. At first I read them merely so as to avoid going to sleep, but afterwards I examined them with more attention, and subsequently with actual avidity, for they opened up to me a new, an unexpected, an unknown, an unfamiliar world. New thoughts, added to new impressions, would come pouring into my heart in a rich flood; and the more emotion, the more pain and labour, it cost me to assimilate these new impressions, the dearer did they become to me, and the more gratefully did they stir my soul to its very depths. Crowding into my heart without giving it time even to breathe, they would cause my whole being to become lost in a wondrous chaos. Yet this spiritual ferment was not sufficiently strong wholly to undo me. For that I was too fanciful, and the fact saved me.

With the passing of my mother's illness the midnight meetings and long conversations between myself and Pokrovski came to an end. Only occasionally did we exchange a few words with one another—words, for the most part, that were of little purport or substance, yet words to which it delighted me to apportion their several meanings, their peculiar secret values. My life had now become full—I was happy; I was quietly, restfully happy. Thus did several weeks elapse....

One day the elder Pokrovski came to see us, and chattered in a brisk, cheerful, garrulous sort of way. He laughed, launched out into witticisms, and, finally, resolved the riddle of his transports by informing us that in a week's time it would be his Petinka's birthday, when, in honour of the occasion, he (the father) meant to don a new jacket (as well as new shoes which his wife was going to buy for him), and to come and pay a visit to his son. In short, the old man was perfectly happy, and gossiped about whatsoever first entered his head.

My lover's birthday! Thenceforward, I could not rest by night or day. Whatever might happen, it was my fixed intention to remind Pokrovski of our friendship by giving him a present. But what sort of present? Finally, I decided to give him books. I knew that he had long wanted to possess a complete set of Pushkin's works, in the latest edition; so, I decided to buy Pushkin. My private fund consisted of thirty roubles, earned by handiwork, and designed eventually to procure me a new dress, but at once I dispatched our cook, old Matrena, to ascertain the price of such an edition. Horrors! The price of the eleven volumes, added to extra outlay upon the binding, would amount to at least SIXTY roubles! Where was the money to come from? I thought and thought, yet could not decide. I did not like to resort to my mother. Of course she would help me, but in that case every one in the house would become aware of my gift, and the gift itself would assume the guise of a recompense—of payment for Pokrovski's labours on my behalf during the past year; whereas, I wished to present the gift ALONE, and without the knowledge of anyone. For the trouble that he had taken with me I wished to be his perpetual debtor—to make him no payment at all save my friendship. At length, I thought of a way out of the difficulty.

I knew that of the hucksters in the Gostinni Dvor one could sometimes buy a book—even one that had been little used and was almost entirely new—for a half of its price, provided that one haggled sufficiently over it; wherefore I determined to repair thither. It so happened that, next day, both Anna Thedorovna and ourselves were in want of sundry articles; and since my mother was unwell and Anna lazy, the execution of the commissions devolved upon me, and I set forth with Matrena.

Luckily, I soon chanced upon a set of Pushkin, handsomely bound, and set myself to bargain for it. At first more was demanded than would have been asked of me in a shop; but afterwards—though not without a great deal of trouble on my part, and several feints at departing—I induced the dealer to lower his price, and to limit his demands to ten roubles in silver. How I rejoiced that I had engaged in this bargaining! Poor Matrena could not imagine what had come to me, nor why I so desired to buy books. But, oh horror of horrors! As soon as ever the dealer caught sight of my capital of thirty roubles in notes, he refused to let the Pushkin go for less than the sum he had first named; and though, in answer to my prayers and protestations, he eventually yielded a little, he did so only to the tune of two-and-a-half roubles more than I possessed, while swearing that he was making the concession for my sake alone, since I was "a sweet young lady," and that he would have done so for no one else in the world. To think that only two-and-a-half roubles should still be wanting! I could have wept with vexation. Suddenly an unlooked-for circumstance occurred to help me in my distress.

Not far away, near another table that was heaped with books, I perceived the elder Pokrovski, and a crowd of four or five hucksters plaguing him nearly out of his senses. Each of these fellows was proffering the old man his own particular wares; and while there was nothing that they did not submit for his approval, there was nothing that he wished to buy. The poor old fellow had the air of a man who is receiving a thrashing. What to make of what he was being offered him he did not know. Approaching him, I inquired what he happened to be doing there; whereat the old man was delighted, since he liked me (it may be) no less than he did Petinka.

"I am buying some books, Barbara Alexievna," said he, "I am buying them for my Petinka. It will be his birthday soon, and since he likes books I thought I would get him some."

The old man always expressed himself in a very roundabout sort of fashion, and on the present occasion he was doubly, terribly confused. Of no matter what book he asked the price, it was sure to be one, two, or three roubles. The larger books he could not afford at all; he could only look at them wistfully, fumble their leaves with his finger, turn over the volumes in his hands, and then replace them. "No, no, that is too dear," he would mutter under his breath. "I must go and try somewhere else." Then again he would fall to examining copy-books, collections of poems, and almanacs of the cheaper order.

"Why should you buy things like those?" I asked him. "They are such rubbish!"

"No, no!" he replied. "See what nice books they are! Yes, they ARE nice books!" Yet these last words he uttered so lingeringly that I could see he was ready to weep with vexation at finding the better sorts of books so expensive. Already a little tear was trickling down his pale cheeks and red nose. I inquired whether he had much money on him; whereupon the poor old fellow pulled out his entire stock, wrapped in a piece of dirty newspaper, and consisting of a few small silver coins, with twenty kopecks in copper. At once I seized the lot, and, dragging him off to my huckster, said: "Look here. These eleven volumes of Pushkin are priced at thirty-two-and-a-half roubles, and I have only thirty roubles. Let us add to them these two-and-a-half roubles of yours, and buy the books together, and make them our joint gift." The old man was overjoyed, and pulled out his money en masse; whereupon the huckster loaded him with our common library. Stuffing it into his pockets, as well as filling both arms with it, he departed homewards with his prize, after giving me his word to bring me the books privately on the morrow.

Next day the old man came to see his son, and sat with him, as usual, for about an hour; after which he visited ourselves, wearing on his face the most comical, the most mysterious expression conceivable. Smiling broadly with satisfaction at the thought that he was the possessor of a secret, he informed me that he had stealthily brought the books to our rooms, and hidden them in a corner of the kitchen, under Matrena's care. Next, by a natural transition, the conversation passed to the coming fete-day; whereupon, the old man proceeded to hold forth extensively on the subject of gifts. The further he delved into his thesis, and the more he expounded it, the clearer could I see that on his mind there was something which he could not, dared not, divulge. So I waited and kept silent. The mysterious exaltation, the repressed satisfaction which I had hitherto discerned in his antics and grimaces and left-eyed winks gradually disappeared, and he began to grow momentarily more anxious and uneasy. At length he could contain himself no longer.

"Listen, Barbara Alexievna," he said timidly. "Listen to what I have got to say to you. When his birthday is come, do you take TEN of the books, and give them to him yourself—that is, FOR yourself, as being YOUR share of the gift. Then I will take the eleventh book, and give it to him MYSELF, as being my gift. If we do that, you will have a present for him and I shall have one—both of us alike."

"Why do you not want us to present our gifts together, Zachar Petrovitch?" I asked him.

"Oh, very well," he replied. "Very well, Barbara Alexievna. Only—only, I thought that—"

The old man broke off in confusion, while his face flushed with the exertion of thus expressing himself. For a moment or two he sat glued to his seat.

"You see," he went on, "I play the fool too much. I am forever playing the fool, and cannot help myself, though I know that it is wrong to do so. At home it is often cold, and sometimes there are other troubles as well, and it all makes me depressed. Well, whenever that happens, I indulge a little, and occasionally drink too much. Now, Petinka does not like that; he loses his temper about it, Barbara Alexievna, and scolds me, and reads me lectures. So I want by my gift to show him that I am mending my ways, and beginning to conduct myself better. For a long time past, I have been saving up to buy him a book—yes, for a long time past I have been saving up for it, since it is seldom that I have any money, unless Petinka happens to give me some. He knows that, and, consequently, as soon as ever he perceives the use to which I have put his money, he will understand that it is for his sake alone that I have acted."

My heart ached for the old man. Seeing him looking at me with such anxiety, I made up my mind without delay.

"I tell you what," I said. "Do you give him all the books."

"ALL?" he ejaculated. "ALL the books?"

"Yes, all of them."

"As my own gift?" "Yes, as your own gift."

"As my gift alone?"

"Yes, as your gift alone."

Surely I had spoken clearly enough, yet the old man seemed hardly to understand me.

"Well," said he after reflection, "that certainly would be splendid—certainly it would be most splendid. But what about yourself, Barbara Alexievna?"

"Oh, I shall give your son nothing."

"What?" he cried in dismay. "Are you going to give Petinka nothing—do you WISH to give him nothing?" So put about was the old fellow with what I had said, that he seemed almost ready to renounce his own proposal if only I would give his son something. What a kind heart he had! I hastened to assure him that I should certainly have a gift of some sort ready, since my one wish was to avoid spoiling his pleasure.

"Provided that your son is pleased," I added, "and that you are pleased, I shall be equally pleased, for in my secret heart I shall feel as though I had presented the gift."

This fully reassured the old man. He stopped with us another couple of hours, yet could not sit still for a moment, but kept jumping up from his seat, laughing, cracking jokes with Sasha, bestowing stealthy kisses upon myself, pinching my hands, and making silent grimaces at Anna Thedorovna. At length, she turned him out of the house. In short, his transports of joy exceeded anything that I had yet beheld.

On the festal day he arrived exactly at eleven o'clock, direct from Mass. He was dressed in a carefully mended frockcoat, a new waistcoat, and a pair of new shoes, while in his arms he carried our pile of books. Next we all sat down to coffee (the day being Sunday) in Anna Thedorovna's parlour. The old man led off the meal by saying that Pushkin was a magnificent poet. Thereafter, with a return to shamefacedness and confusion, he passed suddenly to the statement that a man ought to conduct himself properly; that, should he not do so, it might be taken as a sign that he was in some way overindulging himself; and that evil tendencies of this sort led to the man's ruin and degradation. Then the orator sketched for our benefit some terrible instances of such incontinence, and concluded by informing us that for some time past he had been mending his own ways, and conducting himself in exemplary fashion, for the reason that he had perceived the justice of his son's precepts, and had laid them to heart so well that he, the father, had really changed for the better: in proof whereof, he now begged to present to the said son some books for which he had long been setting aside his savings.

As I listened to the old man I could not help laughing and crying in a breath. Certainly he knew how to lie when the occasion required! The books were transferred to his son's room, and arranged upon a shelf, where Pokrovski at once guessed the truth about them. Then the old man was invited to dinner and we all spent a merry day together at cards and forfeits. Sasha was full of life, and I rivalled her, while Pokrovski paid me numerous attentions, and kept seeking an occasion to speak to me alone. But to allow this to happen I refused. Yes, taken all in all, it was the happiest day that I had known for four years.

But now only grievous, painful memories come to my recollection, for I must enter upon the story of my darker experiences. It may be that that is why my pen begins to move more slowly, and seems as though it were going altogether to refuse to write. The same reason may account for my having undertaken so lovingly and enthusiastically a recounting of even the smallest details of my younger, happier days. But alas! those days did not last long, and were succeeded by a period of black sorrow which will close only God knows when!

My misfortunes began with the illness and death of Pokrovski, who was taken worse two months after what I have last recorded in these memoirs. During those two months he worked hard to procure himself a livelihood since hitherto he had had no assured position. Like all consumptives, he never—not even up to his last moment—altogether abandoned the hope of being able to enjoy a long life. A post as tutor fell in his way, but he had never liked the profession; while for him to become a civil servant was out of the question, owing to his weak state of health. Moreover, in the latter capacity he would have had to have waited a long time for his first instalment of salary. Again, he always looked at the darker side of things, for his character was gradually being warped, and his health undermined by his illness, though he never noticed it. Then autumn came on, and daily he went out to business—that is to say, to apply for and to canvass for posts—clad only in a light jacket; with the result that, after repeated soakings with rain, he had to take to his bed, and never again left it. He died in mid-autumn at the close of the month of October.

Throughout his illness I scarcely ever left his room, but waited on him hand and foot. Often he could not sleep for several nights at a time. Often, too, he was unconscious, or else in a delirium; and at such times he would talk of all sorts of things—of his work, of his books, of his father, of myself. At such times I learned much which I had not hitherto known or divined about his affairs. During the early part of his illness everyone in the house looked askance at me, and Anna Thedorovna would nod her head in a meaning manner; but, I always looked them straight in the face, and gradually they ceased to take any notice of my concern for Pokrovski. At all events my mother ceased to trouble her head about it.

Sometimes Pokrovski would know who I was, but not often, for more usually he was unconscious. Sometimes, too, he would talk all night with some unknown person, in dim, mysterious language that caused his gasping voice to echo hoarsely through the narrow room as through a sepulchre; and at such times, I found the situation a strange one. During his last night he was especially lightheaded, for then he was in terrible agony, and kept rambling in his speech until my soul was torn with pity. Everyone in the house was alarmed, and Anna Thedorovna fell to praying that God might soon take him. When the doctor had been summoned, the verdict was that the patient would die with the morning.

That night the elder Pokrovski spent in the corridor, at the door of his son's room. Though given a mattress to lie upon, he spent his time in running in and out of the apartment. So broken with grief was he that he presented a dreadful spectacle, and appeared to have lost both perception and feeling. His head trembled with agony, and his body quivered from head to foot as at times he murmured to himself something which he appeared to be debating. Every moment I expected to see him go out of his mind. Just before dawn he succumbed to the stress of mental agony, and fell asleep on his mattress like a man who has been beaten; but by eight o'clock the son was at the point of death, and I ran to wake the father. The dying man was quite conscious, and bid us all farewell. Somehow I could not weep, though my heart seemed to be breaking.

The last moments were the most harassing and heartbreaking of all. For some time past Pokrovski had been asking for something with his failing tongue, but I had been unable to distinguish his words. Yet my heart had been bursting with grief. Then for an hour he had lain quieter, except that he had looked sadly in my direction, and striven to make some sign with his death-cold hands. At last he again essayed his piteous request in a hoarse, deep voice, but the words issued in so many inarticulate sounds, and once more I failed to divine his meaning. By turns I brought each member of the household to his bedside, and gave him something to drink, but he only shook his head sorrowfully. Finally, I understood what it was he wanted. He was asking me to draw aside the curtain from the window, and to open the casements. Probably he wished to take his last look at the daylight and the sun and all God's world. I pulled back the curtain, but the opening day was as dull and mournful—looking as though it had been the fast-flickering life of the poor invalid. Of sunshine there was none. Clouds overlaid the sky as with a shroud of mist, and everything looked sad, rainy, and threatening under a fine drizzle which was beating against the window-panes, and streaking their dull, dark surfaces with runlets of cold, dirty moisture. Only a scanty modicum of daylight entered to war with the trembling rays of the ikon lamp. The dying man threw me a wistful look, and nodded. The next moment he had passed away.

The funeral was arranged for by Anna Thedorovna. A plain coffin was bought, and a broken-down hearse hired; while, as security for this outlay, she seized the dead man's books and other articles. Nevertheless, the old man disputed the books with her, and, raising an uproar, carried off as many of them as he could—stuffing his pockets full, and even filling his hat. Indeed, he spent the next three days with them thus, and refused to let them leave his sight even when it was time for him to go to church. Throughout he acted like a man bereft of sense and memory. With quaint assiduity he busied himself about the bier—now straightening the candlestick on the dead man's breast, now snuffing and lighting the other candles. Clearly his thoughts were powerless to remain long fixed on any subject. Neither my mother nor Anna Thedorovna were present at the requiem, for the former was ill and the latter was at loggerheads with the old man. Only myself and the father were there. During the service a sort of panic, a sort of premonition of the future, came over me, and I could hardly hold myself upright. At length the coffin had received its burden and was screwed down; after which the bearers placed it upon a bier, and set out. I accompanied the cortege only to the end of the street. Here the driver broke into a trot, and the old man started to run behind the hearse—sobbing loudly, but with the motion of his running ever they wanting with me now? Thedora declares it all to be a trick, and says that in time they will leave me alone. God grant it be so!

B. D.

June 21st

MY OWN, MY DARLING—I wish to write to you, yet know not where to begin. Things are as strange as though we were actually living together. Also I would add that never in my life have I passed such happy days as I am spending at present. 'Tis as though God had blessed me with a home and a family of my own! Yes, you are my little daughter, beloved. But why mention the four sorry roubles that I sent you? You needed them; I know that from Thedora herself, and it will always be a particular pleasure to me to gratify you in anything. It will always be my one happiness in life. Pray, therefore, leave me that happiness, and do not seek to cross me in it. Things are not as you suppose. I have now reached the sunshine since, in the first place, I am living so close to you as almost to be with you (which is a great consolation to my mind), while, in the second place, a neighbour of mine named Rataziaev (the retired official who gives the literary parties) has today invited me to tea. This evening, therefore, there will be a gathering at which we shall discuss literature! Think of that my darling! Well, goodbye now. I have written this without any definite aim in my mind, but solely to assure you of my welfare. Through Theresa I have received your message that you need an embroidered cloak to wear, so I will go and purchase one. Yes, tomorrow I mean to purchase that embroidered cloak, and so give myself the pleasure of having satisfied one of your wants. I know where to go for such a garment. For the time being I remain your sincere friend,

MAKAR DIEVUSHKIN.

June 22nd

MY DEAREST BARBARA ALEXIEVNA—I have to tell you that a sad event has happened in this house—an event to excite one's utmost pity. This morning, about five o'clock, one of Gorshkov's children died of scarlatina, or something of the kind. I have been to pay the parents a visit of condolence, and found them living in the direst poverty and disorder. Nor is that surprising, seeing that the family lives in a single room, with only a screen to divide it for decency's sake. Already the coffin was standing in their midst—a plain but decent shell which had been bought ready-made. The child, they told me, had been a boy of nine, and full of promise. What a pitiful spectacle! Though not weeping, the mother, poor woman, looked broken with grief. After all, to have one burden the less on their shoulders may prove a relief, though there are still two children left—a babe at the breast and a little girl of six! How painful to see these suffering children, and to be unable to help them! The father, clad in an old, dirty frockcoat, was seated on a dilapidated chair. Down his cheeks there were coursing tears—though less through grief than owing to a long-standing affliction of the eyes. He was so thin, too! Always he reddens in the face when he is addressed, and becomes too confused to answer. A little girl, his daughter, was leaning against the coffin—her face looking so worn and thoughtful, poor mite! Do you know, I cannot bear to see a child look thoughtful. On the floor there lay a rag doll, but she was not playing with it as, may happen to enter my head. Yes, I know all this; but if everyone were to become a fine writer, who would there be left to act as copyists?... Whatsoever questions I may put to you in my letters, dearest, I pray you to answer them. I am sure that you need me, that I can be of use to you; and, since that is so, I must not allow myself to be distracted by any trifle. Even if I be likened to a rat, I do not care, provided that that particular rat be wanted by you, and be of use in the world, and be retained in its position, and receive its reward. But what a rat it is!

Enough of this, dearest one. I ought not to have spoken of it, but I lost my temper. Still, it is pleasant to speak the truth sometimes. Goodbye, my own, my darling, my sweet little comforter! I will come to you soon—yes, I will certainly come to you. Until I do so, do not fret yourself. With me I shall be bringing a book. Once more goodbye.—Your heartfelt well-wisher,

MAKAR DIEVUSHKIN.

June 20th

MY DEAREST MAKAR ALEXIEVITCH—I am writing to you post-haste—I am hurrying my utmost to get my work finished in time. What do you suppose is the reason for this? It is because an opportunity has occurred for you to make a splendid purchase. Thedora tells me that a retired civil servant of her acquaintance has a uniform to sell—one cut to regulation pattern and in good repair, as well as likely to go very cheap. Now, DO not tell me that you have not got the money, for I know from your own lips that you HAVE. Use that money, I pray you, and do not hoard it. See what terrible garments you walk about in! They are shameful—they are patched all over! In fact, you have nothing new whatever. That this is so, I know for certain, and I care not WHAT you tell me about it. So listen to me for once, and buy this uniform. Do it for MY sake. Do it to show that you really love me.

You have sent me some linen as a gift. But listen to me, Makar Alexievitch. You are simply ruining yourself. Is it a jest that you should spend so much money, such a terrible amount of money, upon me? How you love to play the spendthrift! I tell you that I do not need it, that such expenditure is unnecessary. I know, I am CERTAIN, that you love me—therefore, it is useless to remind me of the fact with gifts. Nor do I like receiving them, since I know how much they must have cost you. No—put your money to a better use. I beg, I beseech of you, to do so. Also, you ask me to send you a continuation of my memoirs—to conclude them. But I know not how I contrived even to write as much of them as I did; and now I have not the strength to write further of my past, nor the desire to give it a single thought. Such recollections are terrible to me. Most difficult of all is it for me to speak of my poor mother, who left her destitute daughter a prey to villains. My heart runs blood whenever I think of it; it is so fresh in my memory that I cannot dismiss it from my thoughts, nor rest for its insistence, although a year has now elapsed since the events took place. But all this you know.

Also, I have told you what Anna Thedorovna is now intending. She accuses me of ingratitude, and denies the accusations made against herself with regard to Monsieur Bwikov. Also, she keeps sending for me, and telling me that I have taken to evil courses, but that if I will return to her, she will smooth over matters with Bwikov, and force him to confess his fault. Also, she says that he desires to give me a dowry. Away with them all! I am quite happy here with you and good Thedora, whose devotion to me reminds me of my old nurse, long since dead. Distant kinsman though you may be, I pray you always to defend my honour. Other people I do not wish to know, and would gladly forget if I could.... What are

Nature, your descriptions of rural scenes, your analysis of your own feelings—the whole is beautifully written. Alas, I have no such talent! Though I may fill a score of pages, nothing comes of it—I might as well never have put pen to paper. Yes, this I know from experience.

You say, my darling, that I am kind and good, that I could not harm my fellow-men, that I have power to comprehend the goodness of God (as expressed in nature's handiwork), and so on. It may all be so, my dearest one—it may all be exactly as you say. Indeed, I think that you are right. But if so, the reason is that when one reads such a letter as you have just sent me, one's heart involuntarily softens, and affords entrance to thoughts of a graver and weightier order. Listen, my darling; I have something to tell you, my beloved one.

I will begin from the time when I was seventeen years old and first entered the service—though I shall soon have completed my thirtieth year of official activity. I may say that at first I was much pleased with my new uniform; and, as I grew older, I grew in mind, and fell to studying my fellow-men. Likewise I may say that I lived an upright life—so much so that at last I incurred persecution. This you may not believe, but it is true. To think that men so cruel should exist! For though, dearest one, I am dull and of no account, I have feelings like everyone else. Consequently, would you believe it, Barbara, when I tell you what these cruel fellows did to me? I feel ashamed to tell it you—and all because I was of a quiet, peaceful, good-natured disposition!

Things began with "this or that, Makar Alexievitch, is your fault." Then it went on to "I need hardly say that the fault is wholly Makar Alexievitch's." Finally it became "OF COURSE Makar Alexievitch is to blame." Do you see the sequence of things, my darling? Every mistake was attributed to me, until "Makar Alexievitch" became a byword in our department. Also, while making of me a proverb, these fellows could not give me a smile or a civil word. They found fault with my boots, with my uniform, with my hair, with my figure. None of these things were to their taste: everything had to be changed. And so it has been from that day to this. True, I have now grown used to it, for I can grow accustomed to anything (being, as you know, a man of peaceable disposition, like all men of small stature)—yet why should these things be? Whom have I harmed? Whom have I ever supplanted? Whom have I ever traduced to his superiors? No, the fault is that more than once I have asked for an increase of salary. But have I ever CABALLED for it? No, you would be wrong in thinking so, my dearest one. HOW could I ever have done so? You yourself have had many opportunities of seeing how incapable I am of deceit or chicanery.

Why then, should this have fallen to my lot?... However, since you think me worthy of respect, my darling, I do not care, for you are far and away the best person in the world.... What do you consider to be the greatest social virtue? In private conversation Evstafi Ivanovitch once told me that the greatest social virtue might be considered to be an ability to get money to spend. Also, my comrades used jestingly (yes, I know only jestingly) to propound the ethical maxim that a man ought never to let himself become a burden upon anyone. Well, I am a burden upon no one. It is my own crust of bread that I eat; and though that crust is but a poor one, and sometimes actually a maggoty one, it has at least been EARNED, and therefore, is being put to a right and lawful use. What therefore, ought I to do? I know that I can earn but little by my labours as a copyist; yet even of that little I am proud, for it has entailed WORK, and has wrung sweat from my brow. What harm is there in being a copyist? "He is only an amanuensis," people say of me. But what is there so disgraceful in that? My writing is at least legible, neat, and pleasant to look upon—and his Excellency is satisfied with it. Indeed, I transcribe many important documents. At the same time, I know that my writing lacks STYLE, which is why I have never risen in the service. Even to you, my dear one, I write simply and without tricks, but just as a thought and anon causing the sobs to quaver and become broken off. Next he lost his hat, the poor old fellow, yet would not stop to pick it up, even though the rain was beating upon his head, and a wind was rising and the sleet kept stinging and lashing his face. It seemed as though he were impervious to the cruel elements as he ran from one side of the hearse to the other—the skirts of his old greatcoat flapping about him like a pair of wings. From every pocket of the garment protruded books, while in his hand he carried a specially large volume, which he hugged closely to his breast. The passers-by uncovered their heads and crossed themselves as the cortege passed, and some of them, having done so, remained staring in amazement at the poor old man. Every now and then a book would slip from one of his pockets and fall into the mud; whereupon somebody, stopping him, would direct his attention to his loss, and he would stop, pick up the book, and again set off in pursuit of the hearse. At the corner of the street he was joined by a ragged old woman; until at length the hearse turned a corner, and became hidden from my eyes. Then I went home, and threw myself, in a transport of grief, upon my mother's breast—clasping her in my arms, kissing her amid a storm of sobs and tears, and clinging to her form as though in my embraces I were holding my last friend on earth, that I might preserve her from death. Yet already death was standing over her....

June 11th

How I thank you for our walk to the Islands yesterday, Makar Alexievitch! How fresh and pleasant, how full of verdure, was everything! And I had not seen anything green for such a long time! During my illness I used to think that I should never get better, that I was certainly going to die. Judge, then, how I felt yesterday! True, I may have seemed to you a little sad, and you must not be angry with me for that. Happy and light-hearted though I was, there were moments, even at the height of my felicity, when, for some unknown reason, depression came sweeping over my soul. I kept weeping about trifles, yet could not say why I was grieved. The truth is that I am unwell—so much so, that I look at everything from the gloomy point of view. The pale, clear sky, the setting sun, the evening stillness—ah, somehow I felt disposed to grieve and feel hurt at these things; my heart seemed to be over-charged, and to be calling for tears to relieve it. But why should I write this to you? It is difficult for my heart to express itself; still more difficult for it to forego self-expression. Yet possibly you may understand me. Tears and laughter!... How good you are, Makar Alexievitch! Yesterday you looked into my eyes as though you could read in them all that I was feeling—as though you were rejoicing at my happiness. Whether it were a group of shrubs or an alleyway or a vista of water that we were passing, you would halt before me, and stand gazing at my face as though you were showing me possessions of your own. It told me how kind is your nature, and I love you for it. Today I am again unwell, for yesterday I wetted my feet, and took a chill. Thedora also is unwell; both of us are ailing. Do not forget me. Come and see me as often as you can.—Your own,

BARBARA ALEXIEVNA.

June 12th

MY DEAREST BARBARA ALEXIEVNA—I had supposed that you meant to describe our doings of the other day in verse; yet from you there has arrived only a single sheet of writing. Nevertheless, I must say that, little though you have put into your letter, that little is not expressed with rare beauty and grace.

motionless, she stood there with her finger to her lips. Even a bon-bon which the landlady had given her she was not eating. Is it not all sad, sad, Barbara?

MAKAR DIEVUSHKIN.

June 25th

MY BELOVED MAKAR ALEXIEVITCH—I return you your book. In my opinion it is a worthless one, and I would rather not have it in my possession. Why do you save up your money to buy such trash? Except in jest, do such books really please you? However, you have now promised to send me something else to read. I will share the cost of it. Now, farewell until we meet again. I have nothing more to say.

B. D.

June 26th

MY DEAR LITTLE BARBARA—To tell you the truth, I myself have not read the book of which you speak. That is to say, though I began to read it, I soon saw that it was nonsense, and written only to make people laugh. "However," thought I, "it is at least a CHEERFUL work, and so may please Barbara." That is why I sent it you.

Rataziaev has now promised to give me something really literary to read; so you shall soon have your book, my darling. He is a man who reflects; he is a clever fellow, as well as himself a writer—such a writer! His pen glides along with ease, and in such a style (even when he is writing the most ordinary, the most insignificant of articles) that I have often remarked upon the fact, both to Phaldoni and to Theresa. Often, too, I go to spend an evening with him. He reads aloud to us until five o'clock in the morning, and we listen to him. It is a revelation of things rather than a reading. It is charming, it is like a bouquet of flowers—there is a bouquet of flowers in every line of each page. Besides, he is such an approachable, courteous, kind-hearted fellow! What am I compared with him? Why, nothing, simply nothing! He is a man of reputation, whereas I—well, I do not exist at all. Yet he condescends to my level. At this very moment I am copying out a document for him. But you must not think that he finds any DIFFICULTY in condescending to me, who am only a copyist. No, you must not believe the base gossip that you may hear. I do copying work for him simply in order to please myself, as well as that he may notice me—a thing that always gives me pleasure. I appreciate the delicacy of his position. He is a good—a very good—man, and an unapproachable writer.

What a splendid thing is literature, Barbara—what a splendid thing! This I learnt before I had known Rataziaev even for three days. It strengthens and instructs the heart of man.... No matter what there be in the world, you will find it all written down in Rataziaev's works. And so well written down, too! Literature is a sort of picture—a sort of picture or mirror. It connotes at once passion, expression, fine criticism, good learning, and a document. Yes, I have learned this from Rataziaev himself. I can assure you, Barbara, that if only you could be sitting among us, and listening to the talk (while, with the rest of us, you smoked a pipe), and were to hear those present begin to argue and dispute concerning different matters, you would feel of as little account among them as I do; for I myself figure there only as a blockhead, and feel ashamed, since it takes me a whole evening to think of a single word to interpolate—and even then the word will not come! In a case like that a man regrets that, as the proverb has it, he should have reached man's estate but not man's understanding.... What do I do in my spare time? I sleep like a fool, though I would far rather be occupied with something else—say, with eating or writing, since the one is useful to oneself, and the other is beneficial to one's fellows. You should see how much money these fellows contrive to save! How much, for instance, does not Rataziaev lay by? A few days' writing, I am told, can earn him as much as three hundred roubles! Indeed, if a man be a writer of short stories or anything else that is interesting, he can sometimes pocket five hundred roubles, or a thousand, at a time! Think of it, Barbara! Rataziaev has by him a small manuscript of verses, and for it he is asking—what do you think? Seven thousand roubles! Why, one could buy a whole house for that sum! He has even refused five thousand for a manuscript, and on that occasion I reasoned with him, and advised him to accept the five thousand. But it was of no use. "For," said he, "they will soon offer me seven thousand," and kept to his point, for he is a man of some determination.

Suppose, now, that I were to give you an extract from "Passion in Italy" (as another work of his is called). Read this, dearest Barbara, and judge for yourself:

"Vladimir started, for in his veins the lust of passion had welled until it had reached boiling point.

"'Countess,' he cried, 'do you know how terrible is this adoration of mine, how infinite this madness? No! My fancies have not deceived me—I love you ecstatically, diabolically, as a madman might! All the blood that is in your husband's body could never quench the furious, surging rapture that is in my soul! No puny obstacle could thwart the all-destroying, infernal flame which is eating into my exhausted breast! Oh Zinaida, my Zinaida!'

"'Vladimir!' she whispered, almost beside herself, as she sank upon his bosom.

"'My Zinaida!' cried the enraptured Smileski once more.

"His breath was coming in sharp, broken pants. The lamp of love was burning brightly on the altar of passion, and searing the hearts of the two unfortunate sufferers.

"'Vladimir!' again she whispered in her intoxication, while her bosom heaved, her cheeks glowed, and her eyes flashed fire.

"Thus was a new and dread union consummated.

"Half an hour later the aged Count entered his wife's boudoir.

"'How now, my love?' said he. 'Surely it is for some welcome guest beyond the common that you have had the samovar [Tea-urn.] thus prepared?' And he smote her lightly on the cheek."

What think you of THAT, Barbara? True, it is a little too outspoken—there can be no doubt of that; yet how grand it is, how splendid! With your permission I will also quote you an extract from Rataziaev's story, Ermak and Zuleika:

"'You love me, Zuleika? Say again that you love me, you love me!'

"'I DO love you, Ermak,' whispered Zuleika.

"'Then by heaven and earth I thank you! By heaven and earth you have made me happy! You have given me all, all that my tortured soul has for immemorial years been seeking! 'Tis for this that you have led me hither, my guiding star—'tis for this that you have conducted me to the Girdle of Stone! To all the world will I now show my Zuleika, and no man, demon or monster of Hell, shall bid me nay! Oh, if men would but understand the mysterious passions of her tender heart, and see the poem which lurks in each of her little tears! Suffer me to dry those tears with my kisses! Suffer me to drink of those heavenly drops, Oh being who art not of this earth!'

"'Ermak,' said Zuleika, 'the world is cruel, and men are unjust. But LET them drive us from their midst— let them judge us, my beloved Ermak! What has a poor maiden who was reared amid the snows of Siberia to do with their cold, icy, self-sufficient world? Men cannot understand me, my darling, my sweetheart.'

"'Is that so? Then shall the sword of the Cossacks sing and whistle over their heads!' cried Ermak with a furious look in his eyes."

What must Ermak have felt when he learnt that his Zuleika had been murdered, Barbara?—that, taking advantages of the cover of night, the blind old Kouchoum had, in Ermak's absence, broken into the latter's tent, and stabbed his own daughter in mistake for the man who had robbed him of sceptre and crown?

"'Oh that I had a stone whereon to whet my sword!' cried Ermak in the madness of his wrath as he strove to sharpen his steel blade upon the enchanted rock. 'I would have his blood, his blood! I would tear him limb from limb, the villain!'"

Then Ermak, unable to survive the loss of his Zuleika, throws himself into the Irtisch, and the tale comes to an end.

Here, again, is another short extract—this time written in a more comical vein, to make people laugh:

"Do you know Ivan Prokofievitch Zheltopuzh? He is the man who took a piece out of Prokofi Ivanovitch's leg. Ivan's character is one of the rugged order, and therefore, one that is rather lacking in virtue. Yet he has a passionate relish for radishes and honey. Once he also possessed a friend named Pelagea Antonovna. Do you know Pelagea Antonovna? She is the woman who always puts on her petticoat wrong side outwards."

What humour, Barbara—what purest humour! We rocked with laughter when he read it aloud to us. Yes, that is the kind of man he is. Possibly the passage is a trifle over-frolicsome, but at least it is harmless, and contains no freethought or liberal ideas. In passing, I may say that Rataziaev is not only a supreme writer, but also a man of upright life—which is more than can be said for most writers.

What, do you think, is an idea that sometimes enters my head? In fact, what if I myself were to write something? How if suddenly a book were to make its appearance in the world bearing the title of "The Poetical Works of Makar Dievushkin"? What THEN, my angel? How should you view, should you receive, such an event? I may say of myself that never, after my book had appeared, should I have the hardihood to show my face on the Nevski Prospect; for would it not be too dreadful to hear every one saying,

"Here comes the literateur and poet, Dievushkin—yes, it is Dievushkin himself." What, in such a case, should I do with my feet (for I may tell you that almost always my shoes are patched, or have just been resoled, and therefore look anything but becoming)? To think that the great writer Dievushkin should walk about in patched footgear! If a duchess or a countess should recognise me, what would she say, poor woman? Perhaps, though, she would not notice my shoes at all, since it may reasonably be supposed that countesses do not greatly occupy themselves with footgear, especially with the footgear of civil service officials (footgear may differ from footgear, it must be remembered). Besides, I should find that the countess had heard all about me, for my friends would have betrayed me to her—Rataziaev among the first of them, seeing that he often goes to visit Countess V., and practically lives at her house. She is said to be a woman of great intellect and wit. An artful dog, that Rataziaev!

But enough of this. I write this sort of thing both to amuse myself and to divert your thoughts. Goodbye now, my angel. This is a long epistle that I am sending you, but the reason is that today I feel in good spirits after dining at Rataziaev's. There I came across a novel which I hardly know how to describe to you. Do not think the worse of me on that account, even though I bring you another book instead (for I certainly mean to bring one). The novel in question was one of Paul de Kock's, and not a novel for you to read. No, no! Such a work is unfit for your eyes. In fact, it is said to have greatly offended the critics of St. Petersburg. Also, I am sending you a pound of bonbons—bought specially for yourself. Each time that you eat one, beloved, remember the sender. Only, do not bite the iced ones, but suck them gently, lest they make your teeth ache. Perhaps, too, you like comfits? Well, write and tell me if it is so. Goodbye, goodbye. Christ watch over you, my darling!—Always your faithful friend,

MAKAR DIEVUSHKIN.

June 27th

MY DEAREST MAKAR ALEXIEVITCH—Thedora tells me that, should I wish, there are some people who will be glad to help me by obtaining me an excellent post as governess in a certain house. What think you, my friend? Shall I go or not? Of course, I should then cease to be a burden to you, and the post appears to be a comfortable one. On the other hand, the idea of entering a strange house appals me. The people in it are landed gentry, and they will begin to ask me questions, and to busy themselves about me. What answers shall I then return? You see, I am now so unused to society—so shy! I like to live in a corner to which I have long grown used. Yes, the place with which one is familiar is always the best. Even if for companion one has but sorrow, that place will still be the best.... God alone knows what duties the post will entail. Perhaps I shall merely be required to act as nursemaid; and in any case, I hear that the governess there has been changed three times in two years. For God's sake, Makar Alexievitch, advise me whether to go or not. Why do you never come near me now? Do let my eyes have an occasional sight of you. Mass on Sundays is almost the only time when we see one another. How retiring you have become! So also have I, even though, in a way, I am your kinswoman. You must have ceased to love me, Makar Alexievitch. I spend many a weary hour because of it. Sometimes, when dusk is falling, I find myself lonely—oh, so lonely! Thedora has gone out somewhere, and I sit here and think, and think, and think. I remember all the past, its joys and its sorrows. It passes before my eyes in detail, it glimmers at me as out of a mist; and as it does so, well-known faces appear, which seem actually to be present with me in this room! Most frequently of all, I see my mother. Ah, the dreams that come to me! I feel that my health is breaking, so weak am I. When this morning I arose, sickness took me until I vomited and vomited. Yes, I feel, I know, that death is approaching. Who will bury me when it has come? Who will visit my tomb? Who will sorrow for me? And now it is in a strange place, in the house of a stranger, that I may have to die! Yes, in a corner which I do not know!... My God, how sad a thing is life!... Why do you send me comfits to eat? Whence do you get the money to buy them? Ah, for God's sake keep the money, keep the money. Thedora has sold a carpet which I have made. She got fifty roubles for it, which is very good—I had expected less. Of the fifty roubles I shall give Thedora three, and with the remainder make myself a plain, warm dress. Also, I am going to make you a waistcoat—to make it myself, and out of good material.

Also, Thedora has brought me a book—"The Stories of Bielkin"—which I will forward you, if you would care to read it. Only, do not soil it, nor yet retain it, for it does not belong to me. It is by Pushkin. Two years ago I read these stories with my mother, and it would hurt me to read them again. If you yourself have any books, pray let me have them—so long as they have not been obtained from Rataziaev. Probably he will be giving you one of his own works when he has had one printed. How is it that his compositions please you so much, Makar Alexievitch? I think them SUCH rubbish!

—Now goodbye. How I have been chattering on! When feeling sad, I always like to talk of something, for it acts upon me like medicine—I begin to feel easier as soon as I have uttered what is preying upon my heart. Good bye, good-bye, my friend—Your own

B. D.

June 28th

MY DEAREST BARBARA ALEXIEVNA—Away with melancholy! Really, beloved, you ought to be ashamed of yourself! How can you allow such thoughts to enter your head? Really and truly you are quite well; really and truly you are, my darling. Why, you are blooming—simply blooming. True, I see a certain touch of pallor in your face, but still you are blooming. A fig for dreams and visions! Yes, for shame, dearest! Drive away those fancies; try to despise them. Why do I sleep so well? Why am I never ailing? Look at ME, beloved. I live well, I sleep peacefully, I retain my health, I can ruffle it with my juniors. In fact, it is a pleasure to see me. Come, come, then, sweetheart! Let us have no more of this. I know that that little head of yours is capable of any fancy—that all too easily you take to dreaming and repining; but for my sake, cease to do so.

Are you to go to these people, you ask me? Never! No, no, again no! How could you think of doing such a thing as taking a journey? I will not allow it—I intend to combat your intention with all my might. I will sell my frockcoat, and walk the streets in my shirt sleeves, rather than let you be in want. But no, Barbara. I know you, I know you. This is merely a trick, merely a trick. And probably Thedora alone is to blame for it. She appears to be a foolish old woman, and to be able to persuade you to do anything. Do not believe her, my dearest. I am sure that you know what is what, as well as SHE does. Eh, sweetheart? She is a stupid, quarrelsome, rubbish-talking old woman who brought her late husband to the grave. Probably she has been plaguing you as much as she did him. No, no, dearest; you must not take this step. What should I do then? What would there be left for ME to do? Pray put the idea out of your head. What is it you lack here? I cannot feel sufficiently overjoyed to be near you, while, for your part, you love me well, and can live your life here as quietly as you wish. Read or sew, whichever you like—or read and do not sew. Only, do not desert me. Try, yourself, to imagine how things would seem after you had gone. Here am I sending you books, and later we will go for a walk. Come, come, then, my Barbara! Summon to your aid your reason, and cease to babble of trifles.

As soon as I can I will come and see you, and then you shall tell me the whole story. This will not do, sweetheart; this certainly will not do. Of course, I know that I am not an educated man, and have received but a sorry schooling, and have had no inclination for it, and think too much of Rataziaev, if you will; but he is my friend, and therefore, I must put in a word or two for him. Yes, he is a splendid writer. Again and again I assert that he writes magnificently. I do not agree with you about his works, and never shall. He writes too ornately, too laconically, with too great a wealth of imagery and imagination. Perhaps you have read him without insight, Barbara? Or perhaps you were out of spirits at the time, or angry with Thedora about something, or worried about some mischance? Ah, but you should read him sympathetically, and, best of all, at a time when you are feeling happy and contented and pleasantly disposed—for instance, when you have a bonbon or two in your mouth. Yes, that is the way to read Rataziaev. I do not dispute (indeed, who would do so?) that better writers than he exist—even far better; but they are good, and he is good too—they write well, and he writes well. It is chiefly for his own sake that he writes, and he is to be approved for so doing.

Now goodbye, dearest. More I cannot write, for I must hurry away to business. Be of good cheer, and the Lord God watch over you!—Your faithful friend,

MAKAR DIEVUSHKIN.

P.S—Thank you so much for the book, darling! I will read it through, this volume of Pushkin, and tonight come to you.

MY DEAR MAKAR ALEXIEVITCH—No, no, my friend, I must not go on living near you. I have been thinking the matter over, and come to the conclusion that I should be doing very wrong to refuse so good a post. I should at least have an assured crust of bread; I might at least set to work to earn my employers' favour, and even try to change my character if required to do so. Of course it is a sad and sorry thing to have to live among strangers, and to be forced to seek their patronage, and to conceal and constrain one's own personality—but God will help me. I must not remain forever a recluse, for similar chances have come my way before. I remember how, when a little girl at school, I used to go home on Sundays and spend the time in frisking and dancing about. Sometimes my mother would chide me for so doing, but I did not care, for my heart was too joyous, and my spirits too buoyant, for that. Yet as the evening of Sunday came on, a sadness as of death would overtake me, for at nine o'clock I had to return to school, where everything was cold and strange and severe—where the governesses, on Mondays, lost their tempers, and nipped my ears, and made me cry. On such occasions I would retire to a corner and weep alone; concealing my tears lest I should be called lazy. Yet it was not because I had to study that I used to weep, and in time I grew more used to things, and, after my schooldays were over, shed tears only when I was parting with friends....

It is not right for me to live in dependence upon you. The thought tortures me. I tell you this frankly, for the reason that frankness with you has become a habit. Cannot I see that daily, at earliest dawn, Thedora rises to do washing and scrubbing, and remains working at it until late at night, even though her poor old bones must be aching for want of rest? Cannot I also see that YOU are ruining yourself for me, and hoarding your last kopeck that you may spend it on my behalf? You ought not so to act, my friend, even though you write that you would rather sell your all than let me want for anything. I believe in you, my friend—I entirely believe in your good heart; but, you say that to me now (when, perhaps, you have received some unexpected sum or gratuity) and there is still the future to be thought of. You yourself know that I am always ailing—that I cannot work as you do, glad though I should be of any work if I could get it; so what else is there for me to do? To sit and repine as I watch you and Thedora? But how would that be of any use to you? AM I necessary to you, comrade of mine? HAVE I ever done you any good? Though I am bound to you with my whole soul, and love you dearly and strongly and wholeheartedly, a bitter fate has ordained that that love should be all that I have to give—that I should be unable, by creating for you subsistence, to repay you for all your kindness. Do not, therefore, detain me longer, but think the matter out, and give me your opinion on it. In expectation of which I remain your sweetheart,

B. D.

July 1st

Rubbish, rubbish, Barbara!—What you say is sheer rubbish. Stay here, rather, and put such thoughts out of your head. None of what you suppose is true. I can see for myself that it is not. Whatsoever you lack here, you have but to ask me for it. Here you love and are loved, and we might easily be happy and contented together. What could you want more? What have you to do with strangers? You cannot possibly know what strangers are like. I know it, though, and could have told you if you had asked me. There is a stranger whom I know, and whose bread I have eaten. He is a cruel man, Barbara—a man so bad that he would be unworthy of your little heart, and would soon tear it to pieces with his railings and reproaches and black looks. On the other hand, you are safe and well here—you are as safe as though you were sheltered in a nest. Besides, you would, as it were, leave me with my head gone. For what should I have to do when you were gone? What could I, an old man, find to do? Are you not necessary to me? Are you not useful to me? Eh? Surely you do not think that you are not useful? You are of great use to me, Barbara, for you exercise a beneficial influence upon my life. Even at this moment, as I think of you, I feel cheered, for always I can write letters to you, and put into them what I am feeling, and receive from you detailed answers.... I have bought you a wardrobe, and also procured you a bonnet; so you see that you have only to give me a commission for it to be executed.... No—in what way are you not useful? What should I do if I were deserted in my old age? What would become of me? Perhaps you never thought of that, Barbara—perhaps you never said to yourself, "How could HE get on without me?" You see, I have grown so accustomed to you. What else would it end in, if you were to go away? Why, in my hiking to the Neva's bank and doing away with myself. Ah, Barbara, darling, I can see that you want me to be taken away to the Volkovo Cemetery in a broken-down old hearse, with some poor outcast of the streets to accompany my coffin as chief mourner, and the gravediggers to heap my body with clay, and depart and leave me there. How wrong of you, how wrong of you, my beloved! Yes, by heavens, how wrong of you! I am returning you your book, little friend; and, if you were to ask of me my opinion of it, I should say that never before in my life had I read a book so splendid. I keep wondering how I have hitherto contrived to remain such an owl. For what have I ever done? From what wilds did I spring into existence? I KNOW nothing—I know simply NOTHING. My ignorance is complete. Frankly, I am not an educated man, for until now I have read scarcely a single book—only "A Portrait of Man" (a clever enough work in its way), "The Boy Who Could Play Many Tunes Upon Bells", and "Ivik's Storks". That is all. But now I have also read "The Station Overseer" in your little volume; and it is wonderful to think that one may live and yet be ignorant of the fact that under one's very nose there may be a book in which one's whole life is described as in a picture. Never should I have guessed that, as soon as ever one begins to read such a book, it sets one on both to remember and to consider and to foretell events. Another reason why I liked this book so much is that, though, in the case of other works (however clever they be), one may read them, yet remember not a word of them (for I am a man naturally dull of comprehension, and unable to read works of any great importance)—although, as I say, one may read such works, one reads such a book as YOURS as easily as though it had been written by oneself, and had taken possession of one's heart, and turned it inside out for inspection, and were describing it in detail as a matter of perfect simplicity. Why, I might almost have written the book myself! Why not, indeed? I can feel just as the people in the book do, and find myself in positions precisely similar to those of, say, the character Samson Virin. In fact, how many good-hearted wretches like Virin are there not walking about amongst us? How easily, too, it is all described! I assure you, my darling, that I almost shed tears when I read that Virin so took to drink as to lose his memory, become morose, and spend whole days over his liquor; as also that he choked with grief and wept bitterly when, rubbing his eyes with his dirty hand, he bethought him of his wandering lamb, his daughter Dunasha! How natural, how natural! You should read the book for yourself. The thing is actually alive. Even I can see that; even I can realise that it is a picture cut from the very life around me. In it I see our own Theresa (to go no further) and the poor Tchinovnik—who is just such a man as this Samson Virin, except for his surname of Gorshkov. The book describes just what might happen to ourselves—to myself in particular. Even a count who lives in the Nevski Prospect or in Naberezhnaia Street might have a similar experience, though he might APPEAR to be different, owing to the fact that his life is cast on a higher plane. Yes, just the same things might happen to him—just the same things.... Here you are wishing to go away and leave us; yet, be careful lest it would not be I who had to pay the penalty of your doing so. For you might ruin both yourself and me. For the love of God, put away these thoughts from you, my darling, and do not torture me in vain. How could you, my poor little unfledged nestling, find yourself food, and defend yourself from misfortune, and ward off the wiles of evil men? Think better of it, Barbara, and pay no more heed to foolish advice and calumny, but read your book again, and read it with attention. It may do you much good.

I have spoken of Rataziaev's "The Station Overseer". However, the author has told me that the work is old-fashioned, since, nowadays, books are issued with illustrations and embellishments of different sorts (though I could not make out all that he said). Pushkin he adjudges a splendid poet, and one who has done honour to Holy Russia. Read your book again, Barbara, and follow my advice, and make an old man happy. The Lord God Himself will reward you. Yes, He will surely reward you.—Your faithful friend,

MAKAR DIEVUSHKIN.

MY DEAREST MAKAR ALEXIEVITCH—Today Thedora came to me with fifteen roubles in silver. How glad was the poor woman when I gave her three of them! I am writing to you in great haste, for I am busy cutting out a waistcoat to send to you—buff, with a pattern of flowers. Also I am sending you a book of stories; some of which I have read myself, particularly one called "The Cloak." ... You invite me to go to the theatre with you. But will it not cost too much? Of course we might sit in the gallery. It is a long time (indeed I cannot remember when I last did so) since I visited a theatre! Yet I cannot help fearing that such an amusement is beyond our means. Thedora keeps nodding her head, and saying that you have taken to living above your income. I myself divine the same thing by the amount which you have spent upon me. Take care, dear friend, that misfortune does not come of it, for Thedora has also informed me of certain rumours concerning your inability to meet your landlady's bills. In fact, I am very anxious about you. Now, goodbye, for I must hasten away to see about another matter—about the changing of the ribands on my bonnet.

P.S.—Do you know, if we go to the theatre, I think that I shall wear my new hat and black mantilla. Will that not look nice?

July 7th

MY DEAREST BARBARA ALEXIEVNA—SO much for yesterday! Yes, dearest, we have both been caught playing the fool, for I have become thoroughly bitten with the actress of whom I spoke. Last night I listened to her with all my ears, although, strangely enough, it was practically my first sight of her, seeing that only once before had I been to the theatre. In those days I lived cheek by jowl with a party of five young men—a most noisy crew—and one night I accompanied them, willy-nilly, to the theatre, though I held myself decently aloof from their doings, and only assisted them for company's sake. How those fellows talked to me of this actress! Every night when the theatre was open, the entire band of them (they always seemed to possess the requisite money) would betake themselves to that place of entertainment, where they ascended to the gallery, and clapped their hands, and repeatedly recalled the actress in question. In fact, they went simply mad over her. Even after we had returned home they would give me no rest, but would go on talking about her all night, and calling her their Glasha, and declaring themselves to be in love with "the canary-bird of their hearts." My defenseless self, too, they would plague about the woman, for I was as young as they. What a figure I must have cut with them on the fourth tier of the gallery! Yet, I never got a sight of more than just a corner of the curtain, but had to content myself with listening. She had a fine, resounding, mellow voice like a nightingale's, and we all of us used to clap our hands loudly, and to shout at the top of our lungs. In short, we came very near to being ejected. On the first occasion I went home walking as in a mist, with a single rouble left in my pocket, and an interval of ten clear days confronting me before next pay-day. Yet, what think you, dearest? The very next day, before going to work, I called at a French perfumer's, and spent my whole remaining capital on some eau-de-Cologne and scented soap! Why I did so I do not know. Nor did I dine at home that day, but kept walking and walking past her windows (she lived in a fourth-storey flat on the Nevski Prospect). At length I returned to my own lodging, but only to rest a short hour before again setting off to the Nevski Prospect and resuming my vigil before her windows. For a month and a half I kept this up—dangling in her train. Sometimes I would hire cabs, and discharge them in view of her abode; until at length I had entirely ruined myself, and got into debt. Then I fell out of love with her—I grew weary of the pursuit.... You see, therefore, to what depths an actress can reduce a decent man. In those days I was young. Yes, in those days I was VERY young.

M. D.

July 8th

MY DEAREST BARBARA ALEXIEVNA—The book which I received from you on the 6th of this month I now hasten to return, while at the same time hastening also to explain matters to you in this accompanying letter. What a misfortune, my beloved, that you should have brought me to such a pass! Our lots in life are apportioned by the Almighty according to our human deserts. To such a one He assigns a life in a general's epaulets or as a privy councillor—to such a one, I say, He assigns a life of command; whereas to another one, He allots only a life of unmurmuring toil and suffering. These things are calculated according to a man's CAPACITY. One man may be capable of one thing, and another of another, and their several capacities are ordered by the Lord God himself. I have now been thirty years in the public service, and have fulfilled my duties irreproachably, remained abstemious, and never been detected in any unbecoming behaviour. As a citizen, I may confess—I confess it freely—I have been guilty of certain shortcomings; yet those shortcomings have been combined with certain virtues. I am respected by my superiors, and even his Excellency has had no fault to find with me; and though I have never been shown any special marks of favour, I know that every one finds me at least satisfactory. Also, my writing is sufficiently legible and clear. Neither too rounded nor too fine, it is a running hand, yet always suitable. Of our staff only Ivan Prokofievitch writes a similar hand. Thus have I lived till the grey hairs of my old age; yet I can think of no serious fault committed. Of course, no one is free from MINOR faults. Everyone has some of them, and you among the rest, my beloved. But in grave or in audacious offences never have I been detected, nor in infringements of regulations, nor in breaches of the public peace. No, never! This you surely know, even as the author of your book must have known it. Yes, he also must have known it when he sat down to write. I had not expected this of you, my Barbara. I should never have expected it.

What? In future I am not to go on living peacefully in my little corner, poor though that corner be I am not to go on living, as the proverb has it, without muddying the water, or hurting any one, or forgetting the fear of the Lord God and of oneself? I am not to see, forsooth, that no man does me an injury, or breaks into my home—I am not to take care that all shall go well with me, or that I have clothes to wear, or that my shoes do not require mending, or that I be given work to do, or that I possess sufficient meat and drink? Is it nothing that, where the pavement is rotten, I have to walk on tiptoe to save my boots? If I write to you overmuch concerning myself, is it concerning ANOTHER man, rather, that I ought to write—concerning HIS wants, concerning HIS lack of tea to drink (and all the world needs tea)? Has it ever been my custom to pry into other men's mouths, to see what is being put into them? Have I ever been known to offend any one in that respect? No, no, beloved! Why should I desire to insult other folks when they are not molesting ME? Let me give you an example of what I mean. A man may go on slaving and slaving in the public service, and earn the respect of his superiors (for what it is worth), and then, for no visible reason at all, find himself made a fool of. Of course he may break out now and then (I am not now referring only to drunkenness), and (for example) buy himself a new pair of shoes, and take pleasure in seeing his feet looking well and smartly shod. Yes, I myself have known what it is to feel like that (I write this in good faith). Yet I am nonetheless astonished that Thedor Thedorovitch should neglect what is being said about him, and take no steps to defend himself. True, he is only a subordinate official, and sometimes loves to rate and scold; yet why should he not do so—why should he not indulge in a little vituperation when he feels like it? Suppose it to be NECESSARY, for FORM'S sake, to scold, and to set everyone right, and to shower around abuse (for, between ourselves, Barbara, our friend cannot get on WITHOUT abuse—so much so that every one humours him, and does things behind his back)? Well, since officials differ in rank, and every official demands that he shall be allowed to abuse his fellow officials in proportion to his rank, it follows that the TONE also of official abuse should become divided into ranks, and thus accord with the natural order of things. All the world is built upon the system that each one of us shall have to yield precedence to some other one, as well as to enjoy a certain power of abusing his fellows. Without such a provision the world could not get on at all, and simple chaos would ensue. Yet I am surprised that our Thedor should continue to overlook insults of the kind that he endures.

Why do I do my official work at all? Why is that necessary? Will my doing of it lead anyone who reads it to give me a greatcoat, or to buy me a new pair of shoes? No, Barbara. Men only read the documents, and then require me to write more. Sometimes a man will hide himself away, and not show his face abroad, for the mere reason that, though he has done nothing to be ashamed of, he dreads the gossip and slandering which are everywhere to be encountered. If his civic and family life have to do with literature, everything will be printed and read and laughed over and discussed; until at length, he hardly dare show his face in the street at all, seeing that he will have been described by report as recognisable through his gait alone! Then, when he has amended his ways, and grown gentler (even though he still continues to be loaded with official work), he will come to be accounted a virtuous, decent citizen who has deserved well of his comrades, rendered obedience to his superiors, wished noone any evil, preserved the fear of God in his heart, and died lamented. Yet would it not be better, instead of letting the poor fellow die, to give him a cloak while yet he is ALIVE—to give it to this same Thedor Thedorovitch (that is to say, to myself)? Yes, 'twere far better if, on hearing the tale of his subordinate's virtues, the chief of the department were to call the deserving man into his office, and then and there to promote him, and to grant him an increase of salary. Thus vice would be punished, virtue would prevail, and the staff of that department would live in peace together. Here we have an example from everyday, commonplace life. How, therefore, could you bring yourself to send me that book, my beloved? It is a badly conceived work, Barbara, and also unreal, for the reason that in creation such a Tchinovnik does not exist. No, again I protest against it, little Barbara; again I protest.—Your most humble, devoted servant,

M. D.

July 27th

MY DEAREST MAKAR ALEXIEVITCH—Your latest conduct and letters had frightened me, and left me thunderstruck and plunged in doubt, until what you have said about Thedor explained the situation. Why despair and go into such frenzies, Makar Alexievitch? Your explanations only partially satisfy me. Perhaps I did wrong to insist upon accepting a good situation when it was offered me, seeing that from my last experience in that way I derived a shock which was anything but a matter for jesting. You say also that your love for me has compelled you to hide yourself in retirement. Now, how much I am indebted to you I realised when you told me that you were spending for my benefit the sum which you are always reported to have laid by at your bankers; but, now that I have learned that you never possessed such a fund, but that, on hearing of my destitute plight, and being moved by it, you decided to spend upon me the whole of your salary—even to forestall it—and when I had fallen ill, actually to sell your clothes—when I learned all this I found myself placed in the harassing position of not knowing how to accept it all, nor what to think of it. Ah, Makar Alexievitch! You ought to have stopped at your first acts of charity—acts inspired by sympathy and the love of kinsfolk, rather than have continued to squander your means upon what was unnecessary. Yes, you have betrayed our friendship, Makar Alexievitch, in that you have not been open with me; and, now that I see that your last coin has been spent upon dresses and bon-bons and excursions and books and visits to the theatre for me, I weep bitter tears for my unpardonable improvidence in having accepted these things without giving so much as a thought to your welfare. Yes, all that you have done to give me pleasure has become converted into a source of grief, and left behind it only useless regret. Of late I have remarked that you were looking depressed; and though I felt fearful that something unfortunate was impending, what has happened would otherwise never have entered my head. To think that your better sense should so play you false, Makar Alexievitch! What will people think of you, and say of you? Who will want to know you? You whom, like everyone else, I have valued for your goodness of heart and modesty and good sense—YOU, I say, have now given way to an unpleasant vice of which you seem never before to have been guilty.

What were my feelings when Thedora informed me that you had been discovered drunk in the street, and taken home by the police? Why, I felt petrified with astonishment—although, in view of the fact that you had failed me for four days, I had been expecting some such extraordinary occurrence. Also, have you thought what your superiors will say of you when they come to learn the true reason of your absence? You say that everyone is laughing at you, that every one has learnED of the bond which exists between us, and that your neighbours habitually refer to me with a sneer. Pay no attention to this, Makar Alexievitch; for the love of God, be comforted. Also, the incident between you and the officers has much alarmed me, although I had heard certain rumours concerning it. Pray explain to me what it means. You write, too, that you have been afraid to be open with me, for the reason that your confessions might lose you my friendship. Also, you say that you are in despair at the thought of being unable to help me in my illness, owing to the fact that you have sold everything which might have maintained me, and preserved me in sickness, as well as that you have borrowed as much as it is possible for you to borrow, and are daily experiencing unpleasantness with your landlady. Well, in failing to reveal all this to me you chose the worse course. Now, however, I know all. You have forced me to recognise that I have been the cause of your unhappy plight, as well as that my own conduct has brought upon myself a twofold measure of sorrow. The fact leaves me thunderstruck, Makar Alexievitch. Ah, friend, an infectious disease is indeed a misfortune, for now we poor and miserable folk must perforce keep apart from one another, lest the infection be increased. Yes, I have brought upon you calamities which never before in your humble, solitary life you had experienced. This tortures and exhausts me more than I can tell to think of.

Write to me quite frankly. Tell me how you came to embark upon such a course of conduct. Comfort, oh, comfort me if you can. It is not self-love that prompts me to speak of my own comforting, but my friendship and love for you, which will never fade from my heart. Goodbye. I await your answer with impatience. You have thought but poorly of me, Makar Alexievitch.—Your friend and lover,

BARBARA DOBROSELOVA.

July 28th

MY PRICELESS BARBARA ALEXIEVNA—What am I to say to you, now that all is over, and we are gradually returning to our old position? You say that you are anxious as to what will be thought of me. Let me tell you that the dearest thing in life to me is my self-respect; wherefore, in informing you of my misfortunes and misconduct, I would add that none of my superiors know of my doings, nor ever will know of them, and that therefore, I still enjoy a measure of respect in that quarter. Only one thing do I fear—I fear gossip. Garrulous though my landlady be, she said but little when, with the aid of your ten roubles, I today paid her part of her account; and as for the rest of my companions, they do not matter at all. So long as I have not borrowed money from them, I need pay them no attention. To conclude my explanations, let me tell you that I value your respect for me above everything in the world, and have found it my greatest comfort during this temporary distress of mine. Thank God, the first shock of things has abated, now that you have agreed not to look upon me as faithless and an egotist simply because I have deceived you. I wish to hold you to myself, for the reason that I cannot bear to part with you, and love you as my guardian angel.... I have now returned to work, and am applying myself diligently to my duties. Also, yesterday Evstafi Ivanovitch exchanged a word or two with me. Yet I will not conceal from you the fact that my debts are crushing me down, and that my wardrobe is in a sorry state. At the same time, these things do not REALLY matter and I would bid you not despair about them. Send me, however, another half-rouble if you can (though that half-rouble will stab me to the heart—stab me with the thought that it is not I who am helping you, but YOU who are helping ME). Thedora has done well to get those fifteen roubles for you. At the moment, fool of an old man that I am, I have no hope of acquiring any more money; but as soon as ever I do so, I will write to you and let you know all about it. What chiefly worries me is the fear of gossip. Goodbye, little angel. I kiss your hands, and beseech you to regain your health. If this is not a detailed letter, the reason is that I must soon be starting for the office, in order that, by strict application to duty, I may make amends for the past. Further information concerning my doings (as well as concerning that affair with the officers) must be deferred until tonight.—Your affectionate and respectful friend,

MAKAR DIEVUSHKIN.

July 28th

DEAREST LITTLE BARBARA—It is YOU who have committed a fault—and one which must weigh heavily upon your conscience. Indeed, your last letter has amazed and confounded me—so much so that, on once more looking into the recesses of my heart, I perceive that I was perfectly right in what I did. Of course I am not now referring to my debauch (no, indeed!), but to the fact that I love you, and to the fact that it is unwise of me to love you—very unwise. You know not how matters stand, my darling. You know not why I am BOUND to love you. Otherwise you would not say all that you do. Yet I am persuaded that it is your head rather than your heart that is speaking. I am certain that your heart thinks very differently.

What occurred that night between myself and those officers I scarcely know, I scarcely remember. You must bear in mind that for some time past I have been in terrible distress—that for a whole month I have been, so to speak, hanging by a single thread. Indeed, my position has been most pitiable. Though I hid myself from you, my landlady was forever shouting and railing at me. This would not have mattered a jot—the horrible old woman might have shouted as much as she pleased—had it not been that, in the first place, there was the disgrace of it, and, in the second place, she had somehow learned of our connection, and kept proclaiming it to the household until I felt perfectly deafened, and had to stop my ears. The point, however, is that other people did not stop their ears, but, on the contrary, pricked them. Indeed, I am at a loss what to do.

Really this wretched rabble has driven me to extremities. It all began with my hearing a strange rumour from Thedora—namely, that an unworthy suitor had been to visit you, and had insulted you with an improper proposal. That he had insulted you deeply I knew from my own feelings, for I felt insulted in an equal degree. Upon that, my angel, I went to pieces, and, losing all self-control, plunged headlong. Bursting into an unspeakable frenzy, I was at once going to call upon this villain of a seducer—though what to do next I knew not, seeing that I was fearful of giving you offence. Ah, what a night of sorrow it was, and what a time of gloom, rain, and sleet! Next, I was returning home, but found myself unable to stand upon my feet. Then Emelia Ilyitch happened to come by. He also is a tchinovnik—or rather, was a tchinovnik, since he was turned out of the service some time ago. What he was doing there at that moment I do not know; I only know that I went with him.... Surely it cannot give you pleasure to read of the misfortunes of your friend—of his sorrows, and of the temptations which he experienced?... On the evening of the third day Emelia urged me to go and see the officer of whom I have spoken, and whose address I had learned from our dvornik. More strictly speaking, I had noticed him when, on a previous occasion, he had come to play cards here, and I had followed him home. Of course I now see that I did wrong, but I felt beside myself when I heard them telling him stories about me. Exactly what happened next I cannot remember. I only remember that several other officers were present as well as he. Or it may be that I saw everything double—God alone knows. Also, I cannot exactly remember what I said. I only remember that in my fury I said a great deal. Then they turned me out of the room, and threw me down the staircase—pushed me down it, that is to say. How I got home you know. That is all. Of course, later I blamed myself, and my pride underwent a fall; but no extraneous person except yourself knows of the affair, and in any case it does not matter. Perhaps the affair is as you imagine it to have been, Barbara? One thing I know for certain, and that is that last year one of our lodgers, Aksenti Osipovitch, took a similar liberty with Peter Petrovitch, yet kept the fact secret, an absolute secret. He called him into his room (I happened to be looking through a crack in the partition-wall), and had an explanation with him in the way that a gentleman should—noone except myself being a witness of the scene; whereas, in my own case, I had no explanation at all. After the scene was over, nothing further transpired between Aksenti Osipovitch and Peter Petrovitch, for the reason that the latter was so desirous of getting on in life that he held his tongue. As a result, they bow and shake hands whenever they meet.... I will not dispute the fact that I have erred most grievously—that I should never dare to dispute, or that I have fallen greatly in my own estimation; but, I think I was fated from birth so to do— and one cannot escape fate, my beloved. Here, therefore, is a detailed explanation of my misfortunes and sorrows, written for you to read whenever you may find it convenient. I am far from well, beloved, and have lost all my gaiety of disposition, but I send you this letter as a token of my love, devotion, and respect, Oh dear lady of my affections.—Your humble servant,

MAKAR DIEVUSHKIN.

July 29th

MY DEAREST MAKAR ALEXIEVITCH—I have read your two letters, and they make my heart ache. See here, dear friend of mine. You pass over certain things in silence, and write about a PORTION only of your misfortunes. Can it be that the letters are the outcome of a mental disorder?... Come and see me, for God's sake. Come today, direct from the office, and dine with us as you have done before. As to how you are living now, or as to what settlement you have made with your landlady, I know not, for you write nothing concerning those two points, and seem purposely to have left them unmentioned. Au revoir, my friend. Come to me today without fail. You would do better ALWAYS to dine here. Thedora is an excellent cook. Goodbye—Your own,

BARBARA DOBROSELOVA.

August 1st

MY DARLING BARBARA ALEXIEVNA—Thank God that He has sent you a chance of repaying my good with good. I believe in so doing, as well as in the sweetness of your angelic heart. Therefore, I will not reproach you. Only I pray you, do not again blame me because in the decline of my life I have played the spendthrift. It was such a sin, was it not?—such a thing to do? And even if you would still have it that the sin was there, remember, little friend, what it costs me to hear such words fall from your lips. Do not be vexed with me for saying this, for my heart is fainting. Poor people are subject to fancies—this is a provision of nature. I myself have had reason to know this. The poor man is exacting. He cannot see God's world as it is, but eyes each passer-by askance, and looks around him uneasily in order that he may listen to every word that is being uttered. May not people be talking of him? How is it that he is so unsightly? What is he feeling at all? What sort of figure is he cutting on the one side or on the other? It is matter of common knowledge, my Barbara, that the poor man ranks lower than a rag, and will never earn the respect of any one. Yes, write about him as you like—let scribblers say what they choose about him—he will ever remain as he was. And why is this? It is because, from his very nature, the poor man has to wear his feelings on his sleeve, so that nothing about him is sacred, and as for his self-respect—! Well, Emelia told me the other day that once, when he had to collect subscriptions, official sanction was demanded for every single coin, since people thought that it would be no use paying their money to a poor man. Nowadays charity is strangely administered. Perhaps it has always been so. Either folk do not know how to administer it, or they are adept in the art—one of the two. Perhaps you did not know this, so I beg to tell it you. And how comes it that the poor man knows, is so conscious of it all? The answer is—by experience. He knows because any day he may see a gentleman enter a restaurant and ask himself, "What shall I have to eat today? I will have such and such a dish," while all the time the poor man will have nothing to eat that day but gruel. There are men, too—wretched busybodies—who walk about merely to see if they can find some wretched tchinovnik or broken-down official who has got toes projecting from his boots or his hair uncut! And when they have found such a one they make a report of the circumstance, and their rubbish gets entered on the file.... But what does it matter to you if my hair lacks the shears? If you will forgive me what may seem to you a piece of rudeness, I declare that the poor man is ashamed of such things with the sensitiveness of a young girl. YOU, for instance, would not care (pray pardon my bluntness) to unrobe yourself before the public eye; and in the same way, the poor man does not like to be pried at or questioned concerning his family relations, and so forth. A man of honour and self-respect such as I am finds it painful and grievous to have to consort with men who would deprive him of both.

Today I sat before my colleagues like a bear's cub or a plucked sparrow, so that I fairly burned with shame. Yes, it hurt me terribly, Barbara. Naturally one blushes when one can see one's naked toes projecting through one's boots, and one's buttons hanging by a single thread! As though on purpose, I seemed, on this occasion, to be peculiarly dishevelled. No wonder that my spirits fell. When I was talking on business matters to Stepan Karlovitch, he suddenly exclaimed, for no apparent reason, "Ah, poor old Makar Alexievitch!" and then left the rest unfinished. But I knew what he had in his mind, and blushed so hotly that even the bald patch on my head grew red. Of course the whole thing is nothing, but it worries me, and leads to anxious thoughts. What can these fellows know about me? God send that they know nothing! But I confess that I suspect, I strongly suspect, one of my colleagues. Let them only betray me! They would betray one's private life for a groat, for they hold nothing sacred.

I have an idea who is at the bottom of it all. It is Rataziaev. Probably he knows someone in our department to whom he has recounted the story with additions. Or perhaps he has spread it abroad in his own department, and thence, it has crept and crawled into ours. Everyone here knows it, down to the last detail, for I have seen them point at you with their fingers through the window. Oh yes, I have seen them do it. Yesterday, when I stepped across to dine with you, the whole crew were hanging out of the window to watch me, and the landlady exclaimed that the devil was in young people, and called you certain unbecoming names. But this is as nothing compared with Rataziaev's foul intention to place us in his books, and to describe us in a satire. He himself has declared that he is going to do so, and other people say the same. In fact, I know not what to think, nor what to decide. It is no use concealing the fact that you and I have sinned against the Lord God.... You were going to send me a book of some sort, to divert my mind—were you not, dearest? What book, though, could now divert me? Only such books as have never existed on earth. Novels are rubbish, and written for fools and for the idle. Believe me, dearest, I know it through long experience. Even should they vaunt Shakespeare to you, I tell you that Shakespeare is rubbish, and proper only for lampoons—Your own,

MAKAR DIEVUSHKIN.

August 2nd

MY DEAREST MAKAR ALEXIEVITCH—Do not disquiet yourself. God will grant that all shall turn out well. Thedora has obtained a quantity of work, both for me and herself, and we are setting about it with a will. Perhaps it will put us straight again. Thedora suspects my late misfortunes to be connected with Anna Thedorovna; but I do not care—I feel extraordinarily cheerful today. So you are thinking of borrowing more money? If so, may God preserve you, for you will assuredly be ruined when the time comes for repayment! You had far better come and live with us here for a little while. Yes, come and take up your abode here, and pay no attention whatever to what your landlady says. As for the rest of your enemies and ill-wishers, I am certain that it is with vain imaginings that you are vexing yourself.... In passing, let me tell you that your style differs greatly from letter to letter. Goodbye until we meet again. I await your coming with impatience—Your own,

B. D.

August 3rd

MY ANGEL, BARBARA ALEXIEVNA—I hasten to inform you, Oh light of my life, that my hopes are rising again. But, little daughter of mine—do you really mean it when you say that I am to indulge in no more borrowings? Why, I could not do without them. Things would go badly with us both if I did so. You are ailing. Consequently, I tell you roundly that I MUST borrow, and that I must continue to do so.

Also, I may tell you that my seat in the office is now next to that of a certain Emelia Ivanovitch. He is not the Emelia whom you know, but a man who, like myself, is a privy councillor, as well as represents, with myself, the senior and oldest official in our department. Likewise he is a good, disinterested soul, and one that is not over-talkative, though a true bear in appearance and demeanour. Industrious, and possessed of a handwriting purely English, his caligraphy is, it must be confessed, even worse than my own. Yes, he is a good soul. At the same time, we have never been intimate with one another. We have done no more than exchange greetings on meeting or parting, borrow one another's penknife if we needed one, and, in short, observe such bare civilities as convention demands. Well, today he said to me, "Makar Alexievitch, what makes you look so thoughtful?" and inasmuch as I could see that he wished me well, I told him all—or, rather, I did not tell him EVERYTHING, for that I do to no man (I have not the heart to do it); I told him just a few scattered details concerning my financial straits. "Then you ought to borrow," said he. "You ought to obtain a loan of Peter Petrovitch, who does a little in that way. I myself once borrowed some money of him, and he charged me fair and light interest." Well, Barbara, my heart leapt within me at these words. I kept thinking and thinking—if only God would put it into the mind of Peter Petrovitch to be my benefactor by advancing me a loan! I calculated that with its aid I might both repay my landlady and assist yourself and get rid of my surroundings (where I can hardly sit down to table without the rascals making jokes about me). Sometimes his Excellency passes our desk in the office. He glances at me, and cannot but perceive how poorly I am dressed. Now, neatness and cleanliness are two of his strongest points. Even though he says nothing, I feel ready to die with shame when he approaches. Well, hardening my heart, and putting my diffidence into my ragged pocket, I approached Peter Petrovitch, and halted before him more dead than alive. Yet I was hopeful, and though, as it turned out, he was busily engaged in talking to Thedosei Ivanovitch, I walked up to him from behind, and plucked at his sleeve. He looked away from me, but I recited my speech about thirty roubles, et cetera, et cetera, of which, at first, he failed to catch the meaning. Even when I had explained matters to him more fully, he only burst out laughing, and said nothing. Again I addressed to him my request; whereupon, asking me what security I could give, he again buried himself in his papers, and went on writing without deigning me even a second glance. Dismay seized me. "Peter Petrovitch," I said, "I can offer you no security," but to this I added an explanation that some salary would, in time, be due to me, which I would make over to him, and account the loan my first debt. At that moment someone called him away, and I had to wait a little. On returning, he began to mend his pen as though he had not even noticed that I was there. But I was for myself this time. "Peter Petrovitch," I continued, "can you not do ANYTHING?" Still he maintained silence, and seemed not to have heard me. I waited and waited. At length I determined to make a final attempt, and plucked him by the sleeve. He muttered something, and, his pen mended, set about his writing. There was nothing for me to do but to depart. He and the rest of them are worthy fellows, dearest—that I do not doubt—but they are also proud, very proud. What have I to do with them? Yet I thought I would write and tell you all about it. Meanwhile Emelia Ivanovitch had been encouraging me with nods and smiles. He is a good soul, and has promised to recommend me to a friend of his who lives in Viborskaia Street and lends money. Emelia declares that this friend will certainly lend me a little; so tomorrow, beloved, I am going to call upon the gentleman in question.... What do you think about it? It would be a pity not to obtain a loan. My landlady is on the point of turning me out of doors, and has refused to allow me any more board. Also, my boots are wearing through, and have lost every button—and I do not possess another pair! Could anyone in a government office display greater shabbiness? It is dreadful, my Barbara—it is simply dreadful!

MAKAR DIEVUSHKIN.

August 4th

MY BELOVED MAKAR ALEXIEVITCH—For God's sake borrow some money as soon as you can. I would not ask this help of you were it not for the situation in which I am placed. Thedora and myself cannot remain any longer in our present lodgings, for we have been subjected to great unpleasantness, and you cannot imagine my state of agitation and dismay. The reason is that this morning we received a visit from an elderly—almost an old—man whose breast was studded with orders. Greatly surprised, I asked him what he wanted (for at the moment Thedora had gone out shopping); whereupon he began to question me as to my mode of life and occupation, and then, without waiting for an answer, informed me that he was uncle to the officer of whom you have spoken; that he was very angry with his nephew for the way in which the latter had behaved, especially with regard to his slandering of me right and left; and that he, the uncle, was ready to protect me from the young spendthrift's insolence. Also, he advised me to have nothing to say to young fellows of that stamp, and added that he sympathised with me as though he were my own father, and would gladly help me in any way he could. At this I blushed in some confusion, but did not greatly hasten to thank him. Next, he took me forcibly by the hand, and, tapping my cheek, said that I was very good-looking, and that he greatly liked the dimples in my face (God only knows what he meant!). Finally he tried to kiss me, on the plea that he was an old man, the brute! At this moment Thedora returned; whereupon, in some confusion, he repeated that he felt a great respect for my modesty and virtue, and that he much wished to become acquainted with me; after which he took Thedora aside, and tried, on some pretext or another, to give her money (though of course she declined it). At last he took himself off—again reiterating his assurances, and saying that he intended to return with some earrings as a present; that he advised me to change my lodgings; and, that he could recommend me a splendid flat which he had in his mind's eye as likely to cost me nothing. Yes, he also declared that he greatly liked me for my purity and good sense; that I must beware of dissolute young men; and that he knew Anna Thedorovna, who had charged him to inform me that she would shortly be visiting me in person. Upon that, I understood all. What I did next I scarcely know, for I had never before found myself in such a position; but I believe that I broke all restraints, and made the old man feel thoroughly ashamed of himself—Thedora helping me in the task, and well-nigh turning him neck and crop out of the tenement. Neither of us doubt that this is Anna Thedorovna's work—for how otherwise could the old man have got to know about us?

Now, therefore, Makar Alexievitch, I turn to you for help. Do not, for God's sake, leave me in this plight. Borrow all the money that you can get, for I have not the wherewithal to leave these lodgings, yet cannot possibly remain in them any longer. At all events, this is Thedora's advice. She and I need at least twenty-five roubles, which I will repay you out of what I earn by my work, while Thedora shall get me additional work from day to day, so that, if there be heavy interest to pay on the loan, you shall not be troubled with the extra burden. Nay, I will make over to you all that I possess if only you will continue to help me. Truly, I grieve to have to trouble you when you yourself are so hardly situated, but my hopes rest upon you, and upon you alone. Goodbye, Makar Alexievitch. Think of me, and may God speed you on your errand!

B.D.

August 4th

MY BELOVED BARBARA ALEXIEVNA—These unlooked-for blows have shaken me terribly, and these strange calamities have quite broken my spirit. Not content with trying to bring you to a bed of sickness, these lickspittles and pestilent old men are trying to bring me to the same. And I assure you that they are succeeding—I assure you that they are. Yet I would rather die than not help you. If I cannot help you I SHALL die; but, to enable me to help you, you must flee like a bird out of the nest where these owls, these birds of prey, are seeking to peck you to death. How distressed I feel, my dearest! Yet how cruel you yourself are! Although you are enduring pain and insult, although you, little nestling, are in agony of spirit, you actually tell me that it grieves you to disturb me, and that you will work off your debt to me with the labour of your own hands! In other words, you, with your weak health, are proposing to kill yourself in order to relieve me to term of my financial embarrassments! Stop a moment, and think what you are saying. WHY should you sew, and work, and torture your poor head with anxiety, and spoil your beautiful eyes, and ruin your health? Why, indeed? Ah, little Barbara, little Barbara! Do you not see that I shall never be any good to you, never any good to you? At all events, I myself see it. Yet I WILL help you in your distress. I WILL overcome every difficulty, I WILL get extra work to do, I WILL copy out manuscripts for authors, I WILL go to the latter and force them to employ me, I WILL so apply myself to the work that they shall see that I am a good copyist (and good copyists, I know, are always in demand).

Thus there will be no need for you to exhaust your strength, nor will I allow you to do so—I will not have you carry out your disastrous intention... Yes, little angel, I will certainly borrow some money. I would rather die than not do so. Merely tell me, my own darling, that I am not to shrink from heavy interest, and I will not shrink from it, I will not shrink from it—nay, I will shrink from nothing. I will ask for forty roubles, to begin with. That will not be much, will it, little Barbara? Yet will any one trust me even with that sum at the first asking? Do you think that I am capable of inspiring confidence at the first glance? Would the mere sight of my face lead any one to form of me a favourable opinion? Have I ever been able, remember you, to appear to anyone in a favourable light? What think you? Personally, I see difficulties in the way, and feel sick at heart at the mere prospect. However, of those forty roubles I mean to set aside twenty-five for yourself, two for my landlady, and the remainder for my own spending. Of course, I ought to give more than two to my landlady, but you must remember my necessities, and see for yourself that that is the most that can be assigned to her. We need say no more about it. For one rouble I shall buy me a new pair of shoes, for I scarcely know whether my old ones will take me to the office tomorrow morning. Also, a new neck-scarf is indispensable, seeing that the old one has now passed its first year; but, since you have promised to make of your old apron not only a scarf, but also a shirt-front, I need think no more of the article in question. So much for shoes and scarves. Next, for buttons. You yourself will agree that I cannot do without buttons; nor is there on my garments a single hem unfrayed. I tremble when I think that some day his Excellency may perceive my untidiness, and say—well, what will he NOT say? Yet I shall never hear what he says, for I shall have expired where I sit—expired of mere shame at the thought of having been thus exposed. Ah, dearest!... Well, my various necessities will have left me three roubles to go on with. Part of this sum I shall expend upon a half-pound of tobacco—for I cannot live without tobacco, and it is nine days since I last put a pipe into my mouth. To tell the truth, I shall buy the tobacco without acquainting you with the fact, although I ought not so to do. The pity of it all is that, while you are depriving yourself of everything, I keep solacing myself with various amenities—which is why I am telling you this, that the pangs of conscience may not torment me. Frankly, I confess that I am in desperate straits—in such straits as I have never yet known. My landlady flouts me, and I enjoy the respect of noone; my arrears and debts are terrible; and in the office, though never have I found the place exactly a paradise, noone has a single word to say to me. Yet I hide, I carefully hide, this from every one. I would hide my person in the same way, were it not that daily I have to attend the office where I have to be constantly on my guard against my fellows. Nevertheless, merely to be able to CONFESS this to you renews my spiritual strength. We must not think of these things, Barbara, lest the thought of them break our courage. I write them down merely to warn you NOT to think of them, nor to torture yourself with bitter imaginings. Yet, my God, what is to become of us? Stay where you are until I can come to you; after which I shall not return hither, but simply disappear. Now I have finished my letter, and must go and shave myself, inasmuch as, when that is done, one always feels more decent, as well as consorts more easily with decency. God speed me! One prayer to Him, and I must be off.

M. DIEVUSHKIN.

August 5th

DEAREST MAKAR ALEXIEVITCH—You must not despair. Away with melancholy! I am sending you thirty kopecks in silver, and regret that I cannot send you more. Buy yourself what you most need until tomorrow. I myself have almost nothing left, and what I am going to do I know not. Is it not dreadful, Makar Alexievitch? Yet do not be downcast—it is no good being that. Thedora declares that it would not be a bad thing if we were to remain in this tenement, since if we left it suspicions would arise, and our enemies might take it into their heads to look for us. On the other hand, I do not think it would be well for us to remain here. If I were feeling less sad I would tell you my reason.

What a strange man you are, Makar Alexievitch! You take things so much to heart that you never know what it is to be happy. I read your letters attentively, and can see from them that, though you worry and disturb yourself about me, you never give a thought to yourself. Yes, every letter tells me that you have a kind heart; but I tell YOU that that heart is overly kind. So I will give you a little friendly advice, Makar Alexievitch. I am full of gratitude towards you—I am indeed full for all that you have done for me, I am most sensible of your goodness; but, to think that I should be forced to see that, in spite of your own troubles (of which I have been the involuntary cause), you live for me alone—you live but for MY joys and MY sorrows and MY affection! If you take the affairs of another person so to heart, and suffer with her to such an extent, I do not wonder that you yourself are unhappy. Today, when you came to see me after office-work was done, I felt afraid even to raise my eyes to yours, for you looked so pale and desperate, and your face had so fallen in. Yes, you were dreading to have to tell me of your failure to borrow money—you were dreading to have to grieve and alarm me; but, when you saw that I came very near to smiling, the load was, I know, lifted from your heart. So do not be despondent, do not give way, but allow more rein to your better sense. I beg and implore this of you, for it will not be long before you see things take a turn for the better. You will but spoil your life if you constantly lament another person's sorrow. Goodbye, dear friend. I beseech you not to be over-anxious about me.

B. D.

August 5th

MY DARLING LITTLE BARBARA—This is well, this is well, my angel! So you are of opinion that the fact that I have failed to obtain any money does not matter? Then I too am reassured, I too am happy on your account. Also, I am delighted to think that you are not going to desert your old friend, but intend to remain in your present lodgings. Indeed, my heart was overcharged with joy when I read in your letter those kindly words about myself, as well as a not wholly unmerited recognition of my sentiments. I say this not out of pride, but because now I know how much you love me to be thus solicitous for my feelings. How good to think that I may speak to you of them! You bid me, darling, not be faint-hearted. Indeed, there is no need for me to be so. Think, for instance, of the pair of shoes which I shall be wearing to the office tomorrow! The fact is that over-brooding proves the undoing of a man—his complete undoing. What has saved me is the fact that it is not for myself that I am grieving, that I am suffering, but for YOU. Nor would it matter to me in the least that I should have to walk through the bitter cold without an overcoat or boots—I could bear it, I could well endure it, for I am a simple man in my requirements; but the point is—what would people say, what would every envious and hostile tongue exclaim, when I was seen without an overcoat? It is for OTHER folk that one wears an overcoat and boots. In any case, therefore, I should have needed boots to maintain my name and reputation; to both of which my ragged footgear would otherwise have spelled ruin. Yes, it is so, my beloved, and you may believe an old man who has had many years of experience, and knows both the world and mankind, rather than a set of scribblers and daubers.

But I have not yet told you in detail how things have gone with me today. During the morning I suffered as much agony of spirit as might have been experienced in a year. 'Twas like this: First of all, I went out to call upon the gentleman of whom I have spoken. I started very early, before going to the office. Rain and sleet were falling, and I hugged myself in my greatcoat as I walked along. "Lord," thought I, "pardon my offences, and send me fulfilment of all my desires;" and as I passed a church I crossed myself, repented of my sins, and reminded myself that I was unworthy to hold communication with the Lord God. Then I retired into myself, and tried to look at nothing; and so, walking without noticing the streets, I proceeded on my way. Everything had an empty air, and everyone whom I met looked careworn and preoccupied, and no wonder, for who would choose to walk abroad at such an early hour, and in such weather? Next a band of ragged workmen met me, and jostled me boorishly as they passed; upon which nervousness overtook me, and I felt uneasy, and tried hard not to think of the money that was my errand. Near the Voskresenski Bridge my feet began to ache with weariness, until I could hardly pull myself along; until presently I met with Ermolaev, a writer in our office, who, stepping aside, halted, and followed me with his eyes, as though to beg of me a glass of vodka. "Ah, friend," thought I, "go YOU to your vodka, but what have I to do with such stuff?" Then, sadly weary, I halted for a moment's rest, and thereafter dragged myself further on my way. Purposely I kept looking about me for something upon which to fasten my thoughts, with which to distract, to encourage myself; but there was nothing. Not a single idea could I connect with any given object, while, in addition, my appearance was so draggled that I felt utterly ashamed of it. At length I perceived from afar a gabled house that was built of yellow wood. This, I thought, must be the residence of the Monsieur Markov whom Emelia Ivanovitch had mentioned to me as ready to lend money on interest. Half unconscious of what I was doing, I asked a watchman if he could tell me to whom the house belonged; whereupon grudgingly, and as though he were vexed at something, the fellow muttered that it belonged to one Markov. Are ALL watchmen so unfeeling? Why did this one reply as he did? In any case I felt disagreeably impressed, for like always answers to like, and, no matter what position one is in, things invariably appear to correspond to it. Three times did I pass the house and walk the length of the street; until the further I walked, the worse became my state of mind. "No, never, never will he lend me anything!" I thought to myself, "He does not know me, and my affairs will seem to him ridiculous, and I shall cut a sorry figure. However, let fate decide for me. Only, let Heaven send that I do not afterwards repent me, and eat out my heart with remorse!" Softly I opened the wicket-gate. Horrors! A great ragged brute of a watch-dog came flying out at me, and foaming at the mouth, and nearly jumping out his skin! Curious is it to note what little, trivial incidents will nearly make a man crazy, and strike terror to his heart, and annihilate the firm purpose with which he has armed himself. At all events, I approached the house more dead than alive, and walked straight into another catastrophe. That is to say, not noticing the slipperiness of the threshold, I stumbled against an old woman who was filling milk-jugs from a pail, and sent the milk flying in every direction! The foolish old dame gave a start and a cry, and then demanded of me whither I had been coming, and what it was I wanted; after which she rated me soundly for my awkwardness. Always have I found something of the kind befall me when engaged on errands of this nature. It seems to be my destiny invariably to run into something. Upon that, the noise and the commotion brought out the mistress of the house—an old beldame of mean appearance. I addressed myself directly to her: "Does Monsieur Markov live here?" was my inquiry. "No," she replied, and then stood looking at me civilly enough. "But what want you with him?" she continued; upon which I told her about Emelia Ivanovitch and the rest of the business. As soon as I had finished, she called her daughter—a barefooted girl in her teens—and told her to summon her father from upstairs. Meanwhile, I was shown into a room which contained several portraits of generals on the walls and was furnished with a sofa, a large table, and a few pots of mignonette and balsam. "Shall I, or shall I not (come weal, come woe) take myself off?" was my thought as I waited there. Ah, how I longed to run away! "Yes," I continued, "I had better come again tomorrow, for the weather may then be better, and I shall not have upset the milk, and these generals will not be looking at me so fiercely." In fact, I had actually begun to move towards the door when Monsieur Markov entered—a grey-headed man with thievish eyes, and clad in a dirty dressing-gown fastened with a belt. Greetings over, I stumbled out something about Emelia Ivanovitch and forty roubles, and then came to a dead halt, for his eyes told me that my errand had been futile. "No." said he, "I have no money. Moreover, what security could you offer?" I admitted that I could offer none, but again added something about Emelia, as well as about my pressing needs. Markov heard me out, and then repeated that he had no money. "Ah," thought I, "I might have known this—I might have foreseen it!" And, to tell the truth, Barbara, I could have wished that the earth had opened under my feet, so chilled did I feel as he said what he did, so numbed did my legs grow as shivers began to run down my back. Thus I remained gazing at him while he returned my gaze with a look which said, "Well now, my friend? Why do you not go since you have no further business to do here?" Somehow I felt conscience-stricken. "How is it that you are in such need of money?" was what he appeared to be asking; whereupon, I opened my mouth (anything rather than stand there to no purpose at all!) but found that he was not even listening. "I have no money," again he said, "or I would lend you some with pleasure." Several times I repeated that I myself possessed a little, and that I would repay any loan from him punctually, most punctually, and that he might charge me what interest he liked, since I would meet it without fail. Yes, at that moment I remembered our misfortunes, our necessities, and I remembered your half-rouble. "No," said he, "I can lend you nothing without security," and clinched his assurance with an oath, the robber!

How I contrived to leave the house and, passing through Viborskaia Street, to reach the Voskresenski Bridge I do not know. I only remember that I felt terribly weary, cold, and starved, and that it was ten o'clock before I reached the office. Arriving, I tried to clean myself up a little, but Sniegirev, the porter, said that it was impossible for me to do so, and that I should only spoil the brush, which belonged to the Government. Thus, my darling, do such fellows rate me lower than the mat on which they wipe their boots! What is it that will most surely break me? It is not the want of money, but the LITTLE worries of life—these whisperings and nods and jeers. Any day his Excellency himself may round upon me. Ah, dearest, my golden days are gone. Today I have spent in reading your letters through; and the reading of them has made me sad. Goodbye, my own, and may the Lord watch over you!

M. DIEVUSHKIN.

P.S.—To conceal my sorrow I would have written this letter half jestingly; but, the faculty of jesting has not been given me. My one desire, however, is to afford you pleasure. Soon I will come and see you, dearest. Without fail I will come and see you.

August 11th

O Barbara Alexievna, I am undone—we are both of us undone! Both of us are lost beyond recall! Everything is ruined—my reputation, my self-respect, all that I have in the world! And you as much as I. Never shall we retrieve what we have lost. I—I have brought you to this pass, for I have become an outcast, my darling. Everywhere I am laughed at and despised. Even my landlady has taken to abusing me. Today she overwhelmed me with shrill reproaches, and abased me to the level of a hearth-brush. And last night, when I was in Rataziaev's rooms, one of his friends began to read a scribbled note which I had written to you, and then inadvertently pulled out of my pocket. Oh beloved, what laughter there arose at the recital! How those scoundrels mocked and derided you and myself! I walked up to them and accused Rataziaev of breaking faith. I said that he had played the traitor. But he only replied that I had been the betrayer in the case, by indulging in various amours. "You have kept them very dark though, Mr. Lovelace!" said he—and now I am known everywhere by this name of "Lovelace." They know EVERYTHING about us, my darling, EVERYTHING—both about you and your affairs and about myself; and when today I was for sending Phaldoni to the bakeshop for something or other, he refused to go, saying that it was not his business. "But you MUST go," said I. "I will not," he replied. "You have not paid my mistress what you owe her, so I am not bound to run your errands." At such an insult from a raw peasant I lost my temper, and called him a fool; to which he retorted in a similar vein. Upon this I thought that he must be drunk, and told him so; whereupon he replied: "WHAT say you that I am? Suppose you yourself go and sober up, for I know that the other day you went to visit a woman, and that you got drunk with her on two grivenniks." To such a pass have things come! I feel ashamed to be seen alive. I am, as it were, a man proclaimed; I am in a worse plight even than a tramp who has lost his passport. How misfortunes are heaping themselves upon me! I am lost—I am lost for ever!

M. D.

August 13th

MY BELOVED MAKAR ALEXIEVITCH—It is true that misfortune is following upon misfortune. I myself scarcely know what to do. Yet, no matter how you may be fairing, you must not look for help from me, for only today I burned my left hand with the iron! At one and the same moment I dropped the iron, made a mistake in my work, and burned myself! So now I can no longer work. Also, these three days past, Thedora has been ailing. My anxiety is becoming positively torturous. Nevertheless, I send you thirty kopecks—almost the last coins that I have left to me, much as I should have liked to have helped you more when you are so much in need. I feel vexed to the point of weeping. Goodbye, dear friend of mine. You will bring me much comfort if only you will come and see me today.

B. D.

August 14th

What is the matter with you, Makar Alexievitch? Surely you cannot fear the Lord God as you ought to do? You are not only driving me to distraction but also ruining yourself with this eternal solicitude for your reputation. You are a man of honour, nobility of character, and self-respect, as everyone knows; yet, at any moment, you are ready to die with shame! Surely you should have more consideration for your grey hairs. No, the fear of God has departed from you. Thedora has told you that it is out of my power to render you anymore help. See, therefore, to what a pass you have brought me! Probably you think it is nothing to me that you should behave so badly; probably you do not realise what you have made me suffer. I dare not set foot on the staircase here, for if I do so I am stared at, and pointed at, and spoken about in the most horrible manner. Yes, it is even said of me that I am "united to a drunkard." What a thing to hear! And whenever you are brought home drunk folk say, "They are carrying in that tchinovnik." THAT is not the proper way to make me help you. I swear that I MUST leave this place, and go and get work as a cook or a laundress. It is impossible for me to stay here. Long ago I wrote and asked you to come and see me, yet you have not come. Truly my tears and prayers must mean NOTHING to you, Makar Alexievitch! Whence, too, did you get the money for your debauchery? For the love of God be more careful of yourself, or you will be ruined. How shameful, how abominable of you! So the landlady would not admit you last night, and you spent the night on the doorstep? Oh, I know all about it. Yet if only you could have seen my agony when I heard the news!... Come and see me, Makar Alexievitch, and we will once more be happy together. Yes, we will read together, and talk of old times, and Thedora shall tell you of her pilgrimages in former days. For God's sake beloved, do not ruin both yourself and me. I live for you alone; it is for your sake alone that I am still here. Be your better self once more—the self which still can remain firm in the face of misfortune. Poverty is no crime; always remember that. After all, why should we despair? Our present difficulties will pass away, and God will right us. Only be brave. I send you two grivenniks for the purchase of some tobacco or anything else that you need; but, for the love of heaven, do not spend the money foolishly. Come you and see me soon; come without fail. Perhaps you may be ashamed to meet me, as you were before, but you NEED not feel like that—such shame would be misplaced. Only do bring with you sincere repentance and trust in God, who orders all things for the best.

B. D.

August 19th

MY DEAREST BARBARA ALEXIEVNA,-Yes, I AM ashamed to meet you, my darling—I AM ashamed. At the same time, what is there in all this? Why should we not be cheerful again? Why should I mind the soles of my feet coming through my boots? The sole of one's foot is a mere bagatelle—it will never be anything but just a base, dirty sole. And shoes do not matter, either. The Greek sages used to walk about without them, so why should we coddle ourselves with such things? Yet why, also, should I be insulted and despised because of them? Tell Thedora that she is a rubbishy, tiresome, gabbling old woman, as well as an inexpressibly foolish one. As for my grey hairs, you are quite wrong about them, inasmuch as I am not such an old man as you think. Emelia sends you his greeting. You write that you are in great distress, and have been weeping. Well, I too am in great distress, and have been weeping. Nay, nay. I wish you the best of health and happiness, even as I am well and happy myself, so long as I may remain, my darling—Your friend,

MAKAR DIEVUSHKIN.

August 21st

MY DEAR AND KIND BARBARA ALEXIEVNA—I feel that I am guilty, I feel that I have sinned against you. Yet also I feel, from what you say, that it is no use for me so to feel. Even before I had sinned I felt as I do now; but I gave way to despair, and the more so as recognised my fault. Darling, I am not cruel or hardhearted. To rend your little soul would be the act of a blood-thirsty tiger, whereas I have the heart of a sheep. You yourself know that I am not addicted to bloodthirstiness, and therefore that I cannot really be guilty of the fault in question, seeing that neither my mind nor my heart have participated in it.

Nor can I understand wherein the guilt lies. To me it is all a mystery. When you sent me those thirty kopecks, and thereafter those two grivenniks, my heart sank within me as I looked at the poor little money. To think that though you had burned your hand, and would soon be hungry, you could write to me that I was to buy tobacco! What was I to do? Remorselessly to rob you, an orphan, as any brigand might do? I felt greatly depressed, dearest. That is to say, persuaded that I should never do any good with my life, and that I was inferior even to the sole of my own boot, I took it into my head that it was absurd for me to aspire at all—rather, that I ought to account myself a disgrace and an abomination. Once a man has lost his self-respect, and has decided to abjure his better qualities and human dignity, he falls headlong, and cannot choose but do so. It is decreed of fate, and therefore I am not guilty in this respect.

That evening I went out merely to get a breath of fresh air, but one thing followed another—the weather was cold, all nature was looking mournful, and I had fallen in with Emelia. This man had spent everything that he possessed, and, at the time I met him, had not for two days tasted a crust of bread. He had tried to raise money by pawning, but what articles he had for the purpose had been refused by the pawnbrokers. It was more from sympathy for a fellow-man than from any liking for the individual that I yielded. That is how the fault arose, dearest.

He spoke of you, and I mingled my tears with his. Yes, he is a man of kind, kind heart—a man of deep feeling. I often feel as he did, dearest, and, in addition, I know how beholden to you I am. As soon as ever I got to know you I began both to realise myself and to love you; for until you came into my life I had been a lonely man—I had been, as it were, asleep rather than alive. In former days my rascally colleagues used to tell me that I was unfit even to be seen; in fact, they so disliked me that at length I began to dislike myself, for, being frequently told that I was stupid, I began to believe that I really was so. But the instant that YOU came into my life, you lightened the dark places in it, you lightened both my heart and my soul. Gradually, I gained rest of spirit, until I had come to see that I was no worse than other men, and that, though I had neither style nor brilliancy nor polish, I was still a MAN as regards my thoughts and feelings. But now, alas! pursued and scorned of fate, I have again allowed myself to abjure my own dignity. Oppressed of misfortune, I have lost my courage. Here is my confession to you, dearest. With tears I beseech you not to inquire further into the matter, for my heart is breaking, and life has grown indeed hard and bitter for me—Beloved, I offer you my respect, and remain ever your faithful friend,

MAKAR DIEVUSHKIN.

September 3rd

The reason why I did not finish my last letter, Makar Alexievitch, was that I found it so difficult to write. There are moments when I am glad to be alone—to grieve and repine without any one to share my sorrow: and those moments are beginning to come upon me with ever-increasing frequency. Always in my reminiscences I find something which is inexplicable, yet strongly attractive—so much so that for hours together I remain insensible to my surroundings, oblivious of reality. Indeed, in my present life there is not a single impression that I encounter—pleasant or the reverse—which does not recall to my mind something of a similar nature in the past. More particularly is this the case with regard to my childhood, my golden childhood. Yet such moments always leave me depressed. They render me weak, and exhaust my powers of fancy; with the result that my health, already not good, grows steadily worse.

However, this morning it is a fine, fresh, cloudless day, such as we seldom get in autumn. The air has revived me and I greet it with joy. Yet to think that already the fall of the year has come! How I used to love the country in autumn! Then but a child, I was yet a sensitive being who loved autumn evenings better than autumn mornings. I remember how beside our house, at the foot of a hill, there lay a large pond, and how the pond—I can see it even now!—shone with a broad, level surface that was as clear as crystal. On still evenings this pond would be at rest, and not a rustle would disturb the trees which grew on its banks and overhung the motionless expanse of water. How fresh it used to seem, yet how cold! The dew would be falling upon the turf, lights would be beginning to shine forth from the huts on the pond's margin, and the cattle would be wending their way home. Then quietly I would slip out of the house to look at my beloved pond, and forget myself in contemplation. Here and there a fisherman's bundle of brushwood would be burning at the water's edge, and sending its light far and wide over the surface. Above, the sky would be of a cold blue colour, save for a fringe of flame-coloured streaks on the horizon that kept turning ever paler and paler; and when the moon had come out there would be wafted through the limpid air the sounds of a frightened bird fluttering, of a bulrush rubbing against its fellows in the gentle breeze, and of a fish rising with a splash. Over the dark water there would gather a thin, transparent mist; and though, in the distance, night would be looming, and seemingly enveloping the entire horizon, everything closer at hand would be standing out as though shaped with a chisel— banks, boats, little islands, and all. Beside the margin a derelict barrel would be turning over and over in the water; a switch of laburnum, with yellowing leaves, would go meandering through the reeds; and a belated gull would flutter up, dive again into the cold depths, rise once more, and disappear into the mist. How I would watch and listen to these things! How strangely good they all would seem! But I was a mere infant in those days—a mere child.

Yes, truly I loved autumn-tide—the late autumn when the crops are garnered, and field work is ended, and the evening gatherings in the huts have begun, and everyone is awaiting winter. Then does everything become more mysterious, the sky frowns with clouds, yellow leaves strew the paths at the edge of the naked forest, and the forest itself turns black and blue—more especially at eventide when damp fog is spreading and the trees glimmer in the depths like giants, like formless, weird phantoms. Perhaps one may be out late, and had got separated from one's companions. Oh horrors! Suddenly one starts and trembles as one seems to see a strange-looking being peering from out of the darkness of a hollow tree, while all the while the wind is moaning and rattling and howling through the forest— moaning with a hungry sound as it strips the leaves from the bare boughs, and whirls them into the air. High over the tree-tops, in a widespread, trailing, noisy crew, there fly, with resounding cries, flocks of birds which seem to darken and overlay the very heavens. Then a strange feeling comes over one, until one seems to hear the voice of some one whispering: "Run, run, little child! Do not be out late, for this place will soon have become dreadful! Run, little child! Run!" And at the words terror will possess one's soul, and one will rush and rush until one's breath is spent—until, panting, one has reached home.

At home, however, all will look bright and bustling as we children are set to shell peas or poppies, and the damp twigs crackle in the stove, and our mother comes to look fondly at our work, and our old nurse, Iliana, tells us stories of bygone days, or terrible legends concerning wizards and dead men. At the recital we little ones will press closer to one another, yet smile as we do so; when suddenly, everyone becomes silent. Surely somebody has knocked at the door?... But nay, nay; it is only the sound of Frolovna's spinning-wheel. What shouts of laughter arise! Later one will be unable to sleep for fear of the strange dreams which come to visit one; or, if one falls asleep, one will soon wake again, and, afraid to stir, lie quaking under the coverlet until dawn. And in the morning, one will arise as fresh as a lark and look at the window, and see the fields overlaid with hoarfrost, and fine icicles hanging from the naked branches, and the pond covered over with ice as thin as paper, and a white steam rising from the surface, and birds flying overhead with cheerful cries. Next, as the sun rises, he throws his glittering beams everywhere, and melts the thin, glassy ice until the whole scene has come to look bright and clear and exhilarating; and as the fire begins to crackle again in the stove, we sit down to the tea-urn, while, chilled with the night cold, our black dog, Polkan, will look in at us through the window, and wag his tail with a cheerful air. Presently, a peasant will pass the window in his cart bound for the forest to cut firewood, and the whole party will feel merry and contented together. Abundant grain lies stored in the byres, and great stacks of wheat are glowing comfortably in the morning sunlight. Everyone is quiet and happy, for God has blessed us with a bounteous harvest, and we know that there will be abundance of food for the wintertide. Yes, the peasant may rest assured that his family will not want for aught. Song and dance will arise at night from the village girls, and on festival days everyone will repair to God's house to thank Him with grateful tears for what He has done.... Ah, a golden time was my time of childhood!...

Carried away by these memories, I could weep like a child. Everything, everything comes back so clearly to my recollection! The past stands out so vividly before me! Yet in the present everything looks dim and dark! How will it all end?—how? Do you know, I have a feeling, a sort of sure premonition, that I am going to die this coming autumn; for I feel terribly, oh so terribly ill! Often do I think of death, yet feel that I should not like to die here and be laid to rest in the soil of St. Petersburg. Once more I have had to take to my bed, as I did last spring, for I have never really recovered. Indeed I feel so depressed! Thedora has gone out for the day, and I am alone. For a long while past I have been afraid to be left by myself, for I keep fancying that there is someone else in the room, and that that someone is speaking to me. Especially do I fancy this when I have gone off into a reverie, and then suddenly awoken from it, and am feeling bewildered. That is why I have made this letter such a long one; for, when I am writing, the mood passes away. Goodbye. I have neither time nor paper left for more, and must close. Of the money which I saved to buy a new dress and hat, there remains but a single rouble; but, I am glad that you have been able to pay your landlady two roubles, for they will keep her tongue quiet for a time. And you must repair your wardrobe.

Goodbye once more. I am so tired! Nor can I think why I am growing so weak—why it is that even the smallest task now wearies me? Even if work should come my way, how am I to do it? That is what worries me above all things.

B. D.

September 5th

MY BELOVED BARBARA—Today I have undergone a variety of experiences. In the first place, my head has been aching, and towards evening I went out to get a breath of fresh air along the Fontanka Canal. The weather was dull and damp, and even by six o'clock, darkness had begun to set in. True, rain was not actually falling, but only a mist like rain, while the sky was streaked with masses of trailing cloud. Crowds of people were hurrying along Naberezhnaia Street, with faces that looked strange and dejected. There were drunken peasants; snub-nosed old harridans in slippers; bareheaded artisans; cab drivers; every species of beggar; boys; a locksmith's apprentice in a striped smock, with lean, emaciated features which seemed to have been washed in rancid oil; an ex-soldier who was offering penknives and copper rings for sale; and so on, and so on. It was the hour when one would expect to meet no other folk than these. And what a quantity of boats there were on the canal. It made one wonder how they could all find room there. On every bridge were old women selling damp gingerbread or withered apples, and every woman looked as damp and dirty as her wares. In short, the Fontanka is a saddening spot for a walk, for there is wet granite under one's feet, and tall, dingy buildings on either side of one, and wet mist below and wet mist above. Yes, all was dark and gloomy there this evening.

By the time I had returned to Gorokhovaia Street darkness had fallen and the lamps had been lit. However, I did not linger long in that particular spot, for Gorokhovaia Street is too noisy a place. But what sumptuous shops and stores it contains! Everything sparkles and glitters, and the windows are full of nothing but bright colours and materials and hats of different shapes. One might think that they were decked merely for display; but no—people buy these things, and give them to their wives! Yes, it IS a sumptuous place. Hordes of German hucksters are there, as well as quite respectable traders. And the quantities of carriages which pass along the street! One marvels that the pavement can support so many splendid vehicles, with windows like crystal, linings made of silk and velvet, and lacqueys dressed in epaulets and wearing swords! Into some of them I glanced, and saw that they contained ladies of various ages. Perhaps they were princesses and countesses! Probably at that hour such folk would be hastening to balls and other gatherings. In fact, it was interesting to be able to look so closely at a princess or a great lady. They were all very fine. At all events, I had never before seen such persons as I beheld in those carriages....

Then I thought of you. Ah, my own, my darling, it is often that I think of you and feel my heart sink. How is it that YOU are so unfortunate, Barbara? How is it that YOU are so much worse off than other people? In my eyes you are kind-hearted, beautiful, and clever—why, then, has such an evil fate fallen to your lot? How comes it that you are left desolate—you, so good a human being! While to others happiness comes without an invitation at all? Yes, I know—I know it well—that I ought not to say it, for to do so savours of free-thought; but why should that raven, Fate, croak out upon the fortunes of one person while she is yet in her mother's womb, while another person it permits to go forth in happiness from the home which has reared her? To even an idiot of an Ivanushka such happiness is sometimes granted. "You, you fool Ivanushka," says Fate, "shall succeed to your grandfather's money-bags, and eat, drink, and be merry; whereas YOU (such and such another one) shall do no more than lick the dish, since that is all that you are good for." Yes, I know that it is wrong to hold such opinions, but involuntarily the sin of so doing grows upon one's soul. Nevertheless, it is you, my darling, who ought to be riding in one of those carriages. Generals would have come seeking your favour, and, instead of being clad in a humble cotton dress, you would have been walking in silken and golden attire. Then you would not have been thin and wan as now, but fresh and plump and rosy-cheeked as a figure on a sugar-cake. Then should I too have been happy—happy if only I could look at your lighted windows from the street, and watch your shadow—happy if only I could think that you were well and happy, my sweet little bird! Yet how are things in reality? Not only have evil folk brought you to ruin, but there comes also an old rascal of a libertine to insult you! Just because he struts about in a frockcoat, and can ogle you through a gold-mounted lorgnette, the brute thinks that everything will fall into his hands—that you are bound to listen to his insulting condescension! Out upon him! But why is this? It is because you are an orphan, it is because you are unprotected, it is because you have no powerful friend to afford you the decent support which is your due. WHAT do such facts matter to a man or to men to whom the insulting of an orphan is an offence allowed? Such fellows are not men at all, but mere vermin, no matter what they think themselves to be. Of that I am certain. Why, an organ-grinder whom I met in Gorokhovaia Street would inspire more respect than they do, for at least he walks about all day, and suffers hunger—at least he looks for a stray, superfluous groat to earn him subsistence, and is, therefore, a true gentleman, in that he supports himself. To beg alms he would be ashamed; and, moreover, he works for the benefit of mankind just as does a factory machine. "So far as in me lies," says he, "I will give you pleasure." True, he is a pauper, and nothing but a pauper; but, at least he is an HONOURABLE pauper. Though tired and hungry, he still goes on working—working in his own peculiar fashion, yet still doing honest labour. Yes, many a decent fellow whose labour may be disproportionate to its utility pulls the forelock to no one, and begs his bread of no one. I myself resemble that organ-grinder. That is to say, though not exactly he, I resemble him in this respect, that I work according to my capabilities, and so far as in me lies. More could be asked of no one; nor ought I to be adjudged to do more.

Apropos of the organ-grinder, I may tell you, dearest, that today I experienced a double misfortune. As I was looking at the grinder, certain thoughts entered my head and I stood wrapped in a reverie. Some cabmen also had halted at the spot, as well as a young girl, with a yet smaller girl who was dressed in rags and tatters. These people had halted there to listen to the organ-grinder, who was playing in front of some one's windows. Next, I caught sight of a little urchin of about ten—a boy who would have been good-looking but for the fact that his face was pinched and sickly. Almost barefooted, and clad only in a shirt, he was standing agape to listen to the music—a pitiful childish figure. Nearer to the grinder a few more urchins were dancing, but in the case of this lad his hands and feet looked numbed, and he kept biting the end of his sleeve and shivering. Also, I noticed that in his hands he had a paper of some sort. Presently a gentleman came by, and tossed the grinder a small coin, which fell straight into a box adorned with a representation of a Frenchman and some ladies. The instant he heard the rattle of the coin, the boy started, looked timidly round, and evidently made up his mind that I had thrown the money; whereupon, he ran to me with his little hands all shaking, and said in a tremulous voice as he proffered me his paper: "Pl-please sign this." I turned over the paper, and saw that there was written on it what is usual under such circumstances. "Kind friends I am a sick mother with three hungry children. Pray help me. Though soon I shall be dead, yet, if you will not forget my little ones in this world, neither will I forget you in the world that is to come." The thing seemed clear enough; it was a matter of life and death. Yet what was I to give the lad? Well, I gave him nothing. But my heart ached for him. I am certain that, shivering with cold though he was, and perhaps hungry, the poor lad was not lying. No, no, he was not lying.

The shameful point is that so many mothers take no care of their children, but send them out, half-clad, into the cold. Perhaps this lad's mother also was a feckless old woman, and devoid of character? Or perhaps she had no one to work for her, but was forced to sit with her legs crossed—a veritable invalid? Or perhaps she was just an old rogue who was in the habit of sending out pinched and hungry boys to deceive the public? What would such a boy learn from begging letters? His heart would soon be rendered callous, for, as he ran about begging, people would pass him by and give him nothing. Yes, their hearts would be as stone, and their replies rough and harsh. "Away with you!" they would say. "You are seeking but to trick us." He would hear that from every one, and his heart would grow hard, and he would shiver in vain with the cold, like some poor little fledgling that has fallen out of the nest. His hands and feet would be freezing, and his breath coming with difficulty; until, look you, he would begin to cough, and disease, like an unclean parasite, would worm its way into his breast until death itself had overtaken him—overtaken him in some foetid corner whence there was no chance of escape. Yes, that is what his life would become.

There are many such cases. Ah, Barbara, it is hard to hear "For Christ's sake!" and yet pass the suppliant by and give nothing, or say merely: "May the Lord give unto you!" Of course, SOME supplications mean nothing (for supplications differ greatly in character). Occasionally supplications are long, drawn-out and drawling, stereotyped and mechanical—they are purely begging supplications. Requests of this kind it is less hard to refuse, for they are purely professional and of long standing. "The beggar is overdoing it," one thinks to oneself. "He knows the trick too well." But there are other supplications which voice a strange, hoarse, unaccustomed note, like that today when I took the poor boy's paper. He had been standing by the kerbstone without speaking to anybody—save that at last to myself he said, "For the love of Christ give me a groat!" in a voice so hoarse and broken that I started, and felt a queer sensation in my heart, although I did not give him a groat. Indeed, I had not a groat on me. Rich folk dislike hearing poor people complain of their poverty. "They disturb us," they say, "and are impertinent as well. Why should poverty be so impertinent? Why should its hungry moans prevent us from sleeping?"

To tell you the truth, my darling, I have written the foregoing not merely to relieve my feelings, but, also, still more, to give you an example of the excellent style in which I can write. You yourself will recognise that my style was formed long ago, but of late such fits of despondency have seized upon me that my style has begun to correspond to my feelings; and though I know that such correspondence gains one little, it at least renders one a certain justice. For not unfrequently it happens that, for some reason or another, one feels abased, and inclined to value oneself at nothing, and to account oneself lower than a dishclout; but this merely arises from the fact that at the time one is feeling harassed and depressed, like the poor boy who today asked of me alms. Let me tell you an allegory, dearest, and do you hearken to it. Often, as I hasten to the office in the morning, I look around me at the city—I watch it awaking, getting out of bed, lighting its fires, cooking its breakfast, and becoming vocal; and at the sight, I begin to feel smaller, as though some one had dealt me a rap on my inquisitive nose. Yes, at such times I slink along with a sense of utter humiliation in my heart. For one would have but to see what is passing within those great, black, grimy houses of the capital, and to penetrate within their walls, for one at once to realise what good reason there is for self-depredation and heart-searching. Of course, you will note that I am speaking figuratively rather than literally.

Let us look at what is passing within those houses. In some dingy corner, perhaps, in some damp kennel which is supposed to be a room, an artisan has just awakened from sleep. All night he has dreamt—IF such an insignificant fellow is capable of dreaming?—about the shoes which last night he mechanically cut out. He is a master-shoemaker, you see, and therefore able to think of nothing but his one subject of interest. Nearby are some squalling children and a hungry wife. Nor is he the only man that has to greet the day in this fashion. Indeed, the incident would be nothing—it would not be worth writing about, save for another circumstance. In that same house ANOTHER person—a person of great wealth-may also have been dreaming of shoes; but, of shoes of a very different pattern and fashion (in a manner of speaking, if you understand my metaphor, we are all of us shoemakers). This, again, would be nothing, were it not that the rich person has no one to whisper in his ear: "Why dost thou think of such things? Why dost thou think of thyself alone, and live only for thyself—thou who art not a shoemaker? THY children are not ailing. THY wife is not hungry. Look around thee. Can'st thou not find a subject more fitting for thy thoughts than thy shoes?" That is what I want to say to you in allegorical language, Barbara. Maybe it savours a little of free-thought, dearest; but, such ideas WILL keep arising in my mind and finding utterance in impetuous speech. Why, therefore, should one not value oneself at a groat as one listens in fear and trembling to the roar and turmoil of the city? Maybe you think that I am exaggerating things—that this is a mere whim of mine, or that I am quoting from a book? No, no, Barbara. You may rest assured that it is not so. Exaggeration I abhor, with whims I have nothing to do, and of quotation I am guiltless.

I arrived home today in a melancholy mood. Sitting down to the table, I had warmed myself some tea, and was about to drink a second glass of it, when there entered Gorshkov, the poor lodger. Already, this morning, I had noticed that he was hovering around the other lodgers, and also seeming to want to speak to myself. In passing I may say that his circumstances are infinitely worse than my own; for, only think of it, he has a wife and children! Indeed, if I were he, I do not know what I should do. Well, he entered my room, and bowed to me with the pus standing, as usual, in drops on his eyelashes, his feet shuffling about, and his tongue unable, at first, to articulate a word. I motioned him to a chair (it was a dilapidated enough one, but I had no other), and asked him to have a glass of tea. To this he demurred—for quite a long time he demurred, but at length he accepted the offer. Next, he was for drinking the tea without sugar, and renewed his excuses, but upon the sugar I insisted. After long resistance and many refusals, he DID consent to take some, but only the smallest possible lump; after which, he assured me that his tea was perfectly sweet. To what depths of humility can poverty reduce a man! "Well, what is it, my good sir?" I inquired of him; whereupon he replied: "It is this, Makar Alexievitch. You have once before been my benefactor. Pray again show me the charity of God, and assist my unfortunate family. My wife and children have nothing to eat. To think that a father should have to say this!" I was about to speak again when he interrupted me. "You see," he continued, "I am afraid of the other lodgers here. That is to say, I am not so much afraid of, as ashamed to address them, for they are a proud, conceited lot of men. Nor would I have troubled even you, my friend and former benefactor, were it not that I know that you yourself have experienced misfortune and are in debt; wherefore, I have ventured to come and make this request of you, in that I know you not only to be kind-hearted, but also to be in need, and for that reason the more likely to sympathise with me in my distress." To this he added an apology for his awkwardness and presumption. I replied that, glad though I should have been to serve him, I had nothing, absolutely nothing, at my disposal. "Ah, Makar Alexievitch," he went on, "surely it is not much that I am asking of you? My-my wife and children are starving. C-could you not afford me just a grivennik?" At that my heart contracted, "How these people put me to shame!" thought I. But I had only twenty kopecks left, and upon them I had been counting for meeting my most pressing requirements. "No, good sir, I cannot," said I. "Well, what you will," he persisted. "Perhaps ten kopecks?" Well I got out my cash-box, and gave him the twenty. It was a good deed. To think that such poverty should exist! Then I had some further talk with him. "How is it," I asked him, "that, though you are in such straits, you have hired a room at five roubles?" He replied that though, when he engaged the room six months ago, he paid three months' rent in advance, his affairs had subsequently turned out badly, and never righted themselves since. You see, Barbara, he was sued at law by a merchant who had defrauded the Treasury in the matter of a contract. When the fraud was discovered the merchant was prosecuted, but the transactions in which he had engaged involved Gorshkov, although the latter had been guilty only of negligence, want of prudence, and culpable indifference to the Treasury's interests. True, the affair had taken place some years ago, but various obstacles had since combined to thwart Gorshkov. "Of the disgrace put upon me," said he to me, "I am innocent. True, I to a certain extent disobeyed orders, but never did I commit theft or embezzlement." Nevertheless the affair lost him his character. He was dismissed the service, and though not adjudged capitally guilty, has been unable since to recover from the merchant a large sum of money which is his by right, as spared to him (Gorshkov) by the legal tribunal. True, the tribunal in question did not altogether believe in Gorshkov, but I do so. The matter is of a nature so complex and crooked that probably a hundred years would be insufficient to unravel it; and, though it has now to a certain extent been cleared up, the merchant still holds the key to the situation. Personally I side with Gorshkov, and am very sorry for him. Though lacking a post of any kind, he still refuses to despair, though his resources are completely exhausted. Yes, it is a tangled affair, and meanwhile he must live, for, unfortunately, another child which has been born to him has entailed upon the family fresh expenses. Also, another of his children recently fell ill and died—which meant yet further expense. Lastly, not only is his wife in bad health, but he himself is suffering from a complaint of long standing. In short, he has had a very great deal to undergo. Yet he declares that daily he expects a favourable issue to his affair—that he has no doubt of it whatever. I am terribly sorry for him, and said what I could to give him comfort, for he is a man who has been much bullied and misled. He had come to me for protection from his troubles, so I did my best to soothe him. Now, goodbye, my darling. May Christ watch over you and preserve your health. Dearest one, even to think of you is like medicine to my ailing soul. Though I suffer for you, I at least suffer gladly.—Your true friend,

MAKAR DIEVUSHKIN.

September 9th

MY DEAREST BARBARA ALEXIEVNA—I am beside myself as I take up my pen, for a most terrible thing has happened. My head is whirling round. Ah, beloved, how am I to tell you about it all? I had never foreseen what has happened. But no—I cannot say that I had NEVER foreseen it, for my mind DID get an inkling of what was coming, through my seeing something very similar to it in a dream.

I will tell you the whole story—simply, and as God may put it into my heart. Today I went to the office as usual, and, upon arrival, sat down to write. You must know that I had been engaged on the same sort of work yesterday, and that, while executing it, I had been approached by Timothei Ivanovitch with an urgent request for a particular document. "Makar Alexievitch," he had said, "pray copy this out for me. Copy it as quickly and as carefully as you can, for it will require to be signed today." Also let me tell you, dearest, that yesterday I had not been feeling myself, nor able to look at anything. I had been troubled with grave depression—my breast had felt chilled, and my head clouded. All the while I had been thinking of you, my darling. Well, I set to work upon the copying, and executed it cleanly and well, except for the fact that, whether the devil confused my mind, or a mysterious fate so ordained, or the occurrence was simply bound to happen, I left out a whole line of the document, and thus made nonsense of it! The work had been given me too late for signature last night, so it went before his Excellency this morning. I reached the office at my usual hour, and sat down beside Emelia Ivanovitch. Here I may remark that for a long time past I have been feeling twice as shy and diffident as I used to do; I have been finding it impossible to look people in the face. Let only a chair creak, and I become more dead than alive. Today, therefore, I crept humbly to my seat and sat down in such a crouching posture that Efim Akimovitch (the most touchy man in the world) said to me sotto voce: "What on earth makes you sit like that, Makar Alexievitch?" Then he pulled such a grimace that everyone near us rocked with laughter at my expense. I stopped my ears, frowned, and sat without moving, for I found this the best method of putting a stop to such merriment. All at once I heard a bustle and a commotion and the sound of someone running towards us. Did my ears deceive me? It was I who was being summoned in peremptory tones! My heart started to tremble within me, though I could not say why. I only know that never in my life before had it trembled as it did then. Still I clung to my chair—and at that moment was hardly myself at all. The voices were coming nearer and nearer, until they were shouting in my ear: "Dievushkin! Dievushkin! Where is Dievushkin?" Then at length I raised my eyes, and saw before me Evstafi Ivanovitch. He said to me: "Makar Alexievitch, go at once to his Excellency. You have made a mistake in a document." That was all, but it was enough, was it not? I felt dead and cold as ice—I felt absolutely deprived of the power of sensation; but, I rose from my seat and went whither I had been bidden. Through one room, through two rooms, through three rooms I passed, until I was conducted into his Excellency's cabinet itself. Of my thoughts at that moment I can give no exact account. I merely saw his Excellency standing before me, with a knot of people around him. I have an idea that I did not salute him—that I forgot to do so. Indeed, so panic-stricken was I, that my teeth were chattering and my knees knocking together. In the first place, I was greatly ashamed of my appearance (a glance into a mirror on the right had frightened me with the reflection of myself that it presented), and, in the second place, I had always been accustomed to comport myself as though no such person as I existed. Probably his Excellency had never before known that I was even alive. Of course, he might have heard, in passing, that there was a man named Dievushkin in his department; but never for a moment had he had any intercourse with me.

He began angrily: "What is this you have done, sir? Why are you not more careful? The document was wanted in a hurry, and you have gone and spoiled it. What do you think of it?"—the last being addressed to Evstafi Ivanovitch. More I did not hear, except for some flying exclamations of "What negligence and carelessness! How awkward this is!" and so on. I opened my mouth to say something or other; I tried to beg pardon, but could not. To attempt to leave the room, I had not the hardihood. Then there happened something the recollection of which causes the pen to tremble in my hand with shame. A button of mine—the devil take it!—a button of mine that was hanging by a single thread suddenly broke off, and hopped and skipped and rattled and rolled until it had reached the feet of his Excellency himself—this amid a profound general silence! THAT was what came of my intended self-justification and plea for mercy! THAT was the only answer that I had to return to my chief!

The sequel I shudder to relate. At once his Excellency's attention became drawn to my figure and costume. I remembered what I had seen in the mirror, and hastened to pursue the button. Obstinacy of a sort seized upon me, and I did my best to arrest the thing, but it slipped away, and kept turning over and over, so that I could not grasp it, and made a sad spectacle of myself with my awkwardness. Then there came over me a feeling that my last remaining strength was about to leave me, and that all, all was lost—reputation, manhood, everything! In both ears I seemed to hear the voices of Theresa and Phaldoni. At length, however, I grasped the button, and, raising and straightening myself, stood humbly with clasped hands—looking a veritable fool! But no. First of all I tried to attach the button to the ragged threads, and smiled each time that it broke away from them, and smiled again. In the beginning his Excellency had turned away, but now he threw me another glance, and I heard him say to Evstafi Ivanovitch: "What on earth is the matter with the fellow? Look at the figure he cuts! Who to God is he?" Ah, beloved, only to hear that, "Who to God is he?" Truly I had made myself a marked man! In reply to his Excellency Evstafi murmured: "He is no one of any note, though his character is good. Besides, his salary is sufficient as the scale goes." "Very well, then; but help him out of his difficulties somehow," said his Excellency. "Give him a trifle of salary in advance." "It is all forestalled," was the reply. "He drew it some time ago. But his record is good. There is nothing against him." At this I felt as though I were in Hell fire. I could actually have died! "Well, well," said his Excellency, "let him copy out the document a second time. Dievushkin, come here. You are to make another copy of this paper, and to make it as quickly as possible." With that he turned to some other officials present, issued to them a few orders, and the company dispersed. No sooner had they done so than his Excellency hurriedly pulled out a pocket-book, took thence a note for a hundred roubles, and, with the words, "Take this. It is as much as I can afford. Treat it as you like," placed the money in my hand! At this, dearest, I started and trembled, for I was moved to my very soul. What next I did I hardly know, except that I know that I seized his Excellency by the hand. But he only grew very red, and then—no, I am not departing by a hair's-breadth from the truth—it is true—that he took this unworthy hand in his, and shook it! Yes, he took this hand of mine in his, and shook it, as though I had been his equal, as though I had been a general like himself! "Go now," he said. "This is all that I can do for you. Make no further mistakes, and I will overlook your fault."

What I think about it is this: I beg of you and of Thedora, and had I any children I should beg of them also, to pray ever to God for his Excellency. I should say to my children: "For your father you need not pray; but for his Excellency, I bid you pray until your lives shall end." Yes, dear one—I tell you this in all solemnity, so hearken well unto my words—that though, during these cruel days of our adversity, I have nearly died of distress of soul at the sight of you and your poverty, as well as at the sight of myself and my abasement and helplessness, I yet care less for the hundred roubles which his Excellency has given me than for the fact that he was good enough to take the hand of a wretched drunkard in his own and press it. By that act he restored me to myself. By that act he revived my courage, he made life forever sweet to me.... Yes, sure am I that, sinner though I be before the Almighty, my prayers for the happiness and prosperity of his Excellency will yet ascend to the Heavenly Throne!...

But, my darling, for the moment I am terribly agitated and distraught. My heart is beating as though it would burst my breast, and all my body seems weak.... I send you forty-five roubles in notes. Another twenty I shall give to my landlady, and the remaining thirty-five I shall keep—twenty for new clothes and fifteen for actual living expenses. But these experiences of the morning have shaken me to the core, and I must rest awhile. It is quiet, very quiet, here. My breath is coming in jerks—deep down in my breast I can hear it sobbing and trembling.... I will come and see you soon, but at the moment my head is aching with these various sensations. God sees all things, my darling, my priceless treasure!—Your steadfast friend,

MAKAR DIEVUSHKIN.

September 10th

MY BELOVED MAKAR ALEXIEVITCH—I am unspeakably rejoiced at your good fortune, and fully appreciate the kindness of your superior. Now, take a rest from your cares. Only do not AGAIN spend money to no advantage. Live as quietly and as frugally as possible, and from today begin always to set aside something, lest misfortune again overtake you. Do not, for God's sake, worry yourself—Thedora and I will get on somehow. Why have you sent me so much money? I really do not need it—what I had already would have been quite sufficient. True, I shall soon be needing further funds if I am to leave these lodgings, but Thedora is hoping before long to receive repayment of an old debt. Of course, at least TWENTY roubles will have to be set aside for indispensable requirements, but the remainder shall be returned to you. Pray take care of it, Makar Alexievitch. Now, goodbye. May your life continue peacefully, and may you preserve your health and spirits. I would have written to you at greater length had I not felt so terribly weary. Yesterday I never left my bed. I am glad that you have promised to come and see me. Yes, you MUST pay me a visit.

B. D.

September 11th

MY DARLING BARBARA ALEXIEVNA—I implore you not to leave me now that I am once more happy and contented. Disregard what Thedora says, and I will do anything in the world for you. I will behave myself better, even if only out of respect for his Excellency, and guard my every action. Once more we will exchange cheerful letters with one another, and make mutual confidence of our thoughts and joys and sorrows (if so be that we shall know any more sorrows?). Yes, we will live twice as happily and comfortably as of old. Also, we will exchange books.... Angel of my heart, a great change has taken place in my fortunes—a change very much for the better. My landlady has become more accommodating; Theresa has recovered her senses; even Phaldoni springs to do my bidding. Likewise, I have made my peace with Rataziaev. He came to see me of his own accord, the moment that he heard the glad tidings. There can be no doubt that he is a good fellow, that there is no truth in the slanders that one hears of him. For one thing, I have discovered that he never had any intention of putting me and yourself into a book. This he told me himself, and then read to me his latest work. As for his calling me "Lovelace," he had intended no rudeness or indecency thereby. The term is merely one of foreign derivation, meaning a clever fellow, or, in more literary and elegant language, a gentleman with whom one must reckon. That is all; it was a mere harmless jest, my beloved. Only ignorance made me lose my temper, and I have expressed to him my regret.... How beautiful is the weather today, my little Barbara! True, there was a slight frost in the early morning, as though scattered through a sieve, but it was nothing, and the breeze soon freshened the air. I went out to buy some shoes, and obtained a splendid pair. Then, after a stroll along the Nevski Prospect, I read "The Daily Bee". This reminds me that I have forgotten to tell you the most important thing of all. It happened like this:

This morning I had a talk with Emelia Ivanovitch and Aksenti Michaelovitch concerning his Excellency. Apparently, I am not the only person to whom he has acted kindly and been charitable, for he is known to the whole world for his goodness of heart. In many quarters his praises are to be heard; in many quarters he has called forth tears of gratitude. Among other things, he undertook the care of an orphaned girl, and married her to an official, the son of a poor widow, and found this man place in a certain chancellory, and in other ways benefited him. Well, dearest, I considered it to be my duty to add my mite by publishing abroad the story of his Excellency's gracious treatment of myself. Accordingly, I related the whole occurrence to my interlocutors, and concealed not a single detail. In fact, I put my pride into my pocket—though why should I feel ashamed of having been elated by such an occurrence? "Let it only be noised afield," said I to myself, and it will resound greatly to his Excellency's credit.—So I expressed myself enthusiastically on the subject and never faltered. On the contrary, I felt proud to have such a story to tell. I referred to every one concerned (except to yourself, of course, dearest)—to my landlady, to Phaldoni, to Rataziaev, to Markov. I even mentioned the matter of my shoes! Some of those standing by laughed—in fact every one present did so, but probably it was my own figure or the incident of my shoes—more particularly the latter—that excited merriment, for I am sure it was not meant ill-naturedly. My hearers may have been young men, or well off; certainly they cannot have been laughing with evil intent at what I had said. Anything against his Excellency CANNOT have been in their thoughts. Eh, Barbara?

Even now I cannot wholly collect my faculties, so upset am I by recent events.... Have you any fuel to go on with, Barbara? You must not expose yourself to cold. Also, you have depressed my spirits with your fears for the future. Daily I pray to God on your behalf. Ah, HOW I pray to Him!... Likewise, have you any woollen stockings to wear, and warm clothes generally? Mind you, if there is anything you need, you must not hurt an old man's feelings by failing to apply to him for what you require. The bad times are gone now, and the future is looking bright and fair.

But what bad times they were, Barbara, even though they be gone, and can no longer matter! As the years pass on we shall gradually recover ourselves. How clearly I remember my youth! In those days I never had a kopeck to spare. Yet, cold and hungry though I was, I was always light-hearted. In the morning I would walk the Nevski Prospect, and meet nice-looking people, and be happy all day. Yes, it was a glorious, a glorious time! It was good to be alive, especially in St. Petersburg. Yet it is but yesterday that I was beseeching God with tears to pardon me my sins during the late sorrowful period—to pardon me my murmurings and evil thoughts and gambling and drunkenness. And you I remembered in my prayers, for you alone have encouraged and comforted me, you alone have given me advice and instruction. I shall never forget that, dearest. Today I gave each one of your letters a kiss.... Goodbye, beloved. I have been told that there is going to be a sale of clothing somewhere in this neighbourhood. Once more goodbye, goodbye, my angel—Yours in heart and soul,

MAKAR DIEVUSHKIN.

September 15th

MY DEAREST MAKAR ALEXIEVITCH—I am in terrible distress. I feel sure that something is about to happen. The matter, my beloved friend, is that Monsieur Bwikov is again in St. Petersburg, for Thedora has met him. He was driving along in a drozhki, but, on meeting Thedora, he ordered the coachman to stop, sprang out, and inquired of her where she was living; but this she would not tell him. Next, he said with a smile that he knew quite well who was living with her (evidently Anna Thedorovna had told him); whereupon Thedora could hold out no longer, but then and there, in the street, railed at and abused him—telling him that he was an immoral man, and the cause of all my misfortunes. To this he replied that a person who did not possess a groat must surely be rather badly off; to which Thedora retorted that I could always either live by the labour of my hands or marry—that it was not so much a question of my losing posts as of my losing my happiness, the ruin of which had led almost to my death. In reply he observed that, though I was still quite young, I seemed to have lost my wits, and that my "virtue appeared to be under a cloud" (I quote his exact words). Both I and Thedora had thought that he does not know where I live; but, last night, just as I had left the house to make a few purchases in the Gostinni Dvor, he appeared at our rooms (evidently he had not wanted to find me at home), and put many questions to Thedora concerning our way of living. Then, after inspecting my work, he wound up with: "Who is this tchinovnik friend of yours?" At the moment you happened to be passing through the courtyard, so Thedora pointed you out, and the man peered at you, and laughed. Thedora next asked him to depart—telling him that I was still ill from grief, and that it would give me great pain to see him there; to which, after a pause, he replied that he had come because he had had nothing better to do. Also, he was for giving Thedora twenty-five roubles, but, of course, she declined them. What does it all mean? Why has he paid this visit? I cannot understand his getting to know about me. I am lost in conjecture. Thedora, however, says that Aksinia, her sister-in-law (who sometimes comes to see her), is acquainted with a laundress named Nastasia, and that this woman has a cousin in the position of watchman to a department of which a certain friend of Anna Thedorovna's nephew forms one of the staff. Can it be, therefore, that an intrigue has been hatched through THIS channel? But Thedora may be entirely mistaken. We hardly know what to think. What if he should come again? The very thought terrifies me. When Thedora told me of this last night such terror seized upon me that I almost swooned away. What can the man be wanting? At all events, I refuse to know such people. What have they to do with my wretched self? Ah, how I am haunted with anxiety, for every moment I keep thinking that Bwikov is at hand! WHAT will become of me? WHAT MORE has fate in store for me? For Christ's sake come and see me, Makar Alexievitch! For Christ's sake come and see me soon!

September 18th

MY BELOVED BARBARA ALEXIEVNA—Today there took place in this house a most lamentable, a most mysterious, a most unlooked-for occurrence. First of all, let me tell you that poor Gorshkov has been entirely absolved of guilt. The decision has been long in coming, but this morning he went to hear the final resolution read. It was entirely in his favour. Any culpability which had been imputed to him for negligence and irregularity was removed by the resolution. Likewise, he was authorised to recover of the merchant a large sum of money. Thus, he stands entirely justified, and has had his character cleansed from all stain. In short, he could not have wished for a more complete vindication. When he arrived home at three o'clock he was looking as white as a sheet, and his lips were quivering. Yet there was a smile on his face as he embraced his wife and children. In a body the rest of us ran to congratulate him, and he was greatly moved by the act. Bowing to us, he pressed our hands in turn. As he did so I thought, somehow, that he seemed to have grown taller and straighter, and that the pus-drops seemed to have disappeared from his eyelashes. Yet how agitated he was, poor fellow! He could not rest quietly for two minutes together, but kept picking up and then dropping whatsoever came to his hand, and bowing and smiling without intermission, and sitting down and getting up, and again sitting down, and chattering God only knows what about his honour and his good name and his little ones. How he did talk—yes, and weep too! Indeed, few of ourselves could refrain from tears; although Rataziaev remarked (probably to encourage Gorshkov) that honour mattered nothing when one had nothing to eat, and that money was the chief thing in the world, and that for it alone ought God to be thanked. Then he slapped Gorshkov on the shoulder, but I thought that Gorshkov somehow seemed hurt at this. He did not express any open displeasure, but threw Rataziaev a curious look, and removed his hand from his shoulder. ONCE upon a time he would not have acted thus; but characters differ. For example, I myself should have hesitated, at such a season of rejoicing, to seem proud, even though excessive deference and civility at such a moment might have been construed as a lapse both of moral courage and of mental vigour. However, this is none of my business. All that Gorshkov said was: "Yes, money IS a good thing, glory be to God!" In fact, the whole time that we remained in his room he kept repeating to himself: "Glory be to God, glory be to God!" His wife ordered a richer and more delicate meal than usual, and the landlady herself cooked it, for at heart she is not a bad woman. But until the meal was served Gorshkov could not remain still. He kept entering everyone's room in turn (whether invited thither or not), and, seating himself smilingly upon a chair, would sometimes say something, and sometimes not utter a word, but get up and go out again. In the naval officer's room he even took a pack of playing-cards into his hand, and was thereupon invited to make a fourth in a game; but after losing a few times, as well as making several blunders in his play, he abandoned the pursuit. "No," said he, "that is the sort of man that I am—that is all that I am good for," and departed. Next, encountering myself in the corridor, he took my hands in his, and gazed into my face with a rather curious air. Then he pressed my hands again, and moved away still smiling, smiling, but in an odd, weary sort of manner, much as a corpse might smile. Meanwhile his wife was weeping for joy, and everything in their room was decked in holiday guise. Presently dinner was served, and after they had dined Gorshkov said to his wife: "See now, dearest, I am going to rest a little while;" and with that went to bed. Presently he called his little daughter to his side, and, laying his hand upon the child's head, lay a long while looking at her. Then he turned to his wife again, and asked her: "What of Petinka? Where is our Petinka?" whereupon his wife crossed herself, and replied: "Why, our Petinka is dead!" "Yes, yes, I know—of course," said her husband. "Petinka is now in the Kingdom of Heaven." This showed his wife that her husband was not quite in his right senses—that the recent occurrence had upset him; so she said: "My dearest, you must sleep awhile." "I will do so," he replied, "—at once—I am rather—" And he turned over, and lay silent for a time. Then again he turned round and tried to say something, but his wife could not hear what it was. "What do you say?" she inquired, but he made no reply. Then again she waited a few moments until she thought to herself, "He has gone to sleep," and departed to spend an hour with the landlady. At the end of that hour she returned—only to find that her husband had not yet awoken, but was still lying motionless. "He is sleeping very soundly," she reflected as she sat down and began to work at something or other. Since then she has told us that when half an hour or so had elapsed she fell into a reverie. What she was thinking of she cannot remember, save that she had forgotten altogether about her husband. Then she awoke with a curious sort of sensation at her heart. The first thing that struck her was the deathlike stillness of the room. Glancing at the bed, she perceived her husband to be lying in the same position as before. Thereupon she approached him, turned the coverlet back, and saw that he was stiff and cold—that he had died suddenly, as though smitten with a stroke. But of what precisely he died God only knows. The affair has so terribly impressed me that even now I cannot fully collect my thoughts. It would scarcely be believed that a human being could die so simply—and he such a poor, needy wretch, this Gorshkov! What a fate, what a fate, to be sure! His wife is plunged in tears and panic-stricken, while his little daughter has run away somewhere to hide herself. In their room, however, all is bustle and confusion, for the doctors are about to make an autopsy on the corpse. But I cannot tell you things for certain; I only know that I am most grieved, most grieved. How sad to think that one never knows what even a day, what even an hour, may bring forth! One seems to die to so little purpose!—Your own

MAKAR DIEVUSHKIN.

September 19th

MY BELOVED BARBARA ALEXIEVNA—I hasten to let you know that Rataziaev has found me some work to do for a certain writer—the latter having submitted to him a large manuscript. Glory be to God, for this means a large amount of work to do. Yet, though the copy is wanted in haste, the original is so carelessly written that I hardly know how to set about my task. Indeed, certain parts of the manuscript are almost undecipherable. I have agreed to do the work for forty kopecks a sheet. You see therefore (and this is my true reason for writing to you), that we shall soon be receiving money from an extraneous source. Goodbye now, as I must begin upon my labours.—Your sincere friend,

MAKAR DIEVUSHKIN.

September 23rd

MY DEAREST MAKAR ALEXIEVITCH—I have not written to you these three days past for the reason that I have been so worried and alarmed.

Three days ago Bwikov came again to see me. At the time I was alone, for Thedora had gone out somewhere. As soon as I opened the door the sight of him so terrified me that I stood rooted to the spot, and could feel myself turning pale. Entering with his usual loud laugh, he took a chair, and sat down. For a long while I could not collect my thoughts; I just sat where I was, and went on with my work. Soon his smile faded, for my appearance seemed somehow to have struck him. You see, of late I have grown thin, and my eyes and cheeks have fallen in, and my face has become as white as a sheet; so that anyone who knew me a year ago would scarcely recognise me now. After a prolonged inspection, Bwikov seemed to recover his spirits, for he said something to which I duly replied. Then again he laughed. Thus he sat for a whole hour—talking to me the while, and asking me questions about one thing and another. At length, just before he rose to depart, he took me by the hand, and said (to quote his exact words): "Between ourselves, Barbara Alexievna, that kinswoman of yours and my good friend and acquaintance—I refer to Anna Thedorovna—is a very bad woman," (he also added a grosser term of opprobrium). "First of all she led your cousin astray, and then she ruined yourself. I also have behaved like a villain, but such is the way of the world." Again he laughed. Next, having remarked that, though not a master of eloquence, he had always considered that obligations of gentility obliged him to have with me a clear and outspoken explanation, he went on to say that he sought my hand in marriage; that he looked upon it as a duty to restore to me my honour; that he could offer me riches; that, after marriage, he would take me to his country seat in the Steppes, where we would hunt hares; that he intended never to visit St. Petersburg again, since everything there was horrible, and he had to entertain a worthless nephew whom he had sworn to disinherit in favour of a legal heir; and, finally, that it was to obtain such a legal heir that he was seeking my hand in marriage. Lastly, he remarked that I seemed to be living in very poor circumstances (which was not surprising, said he, in view of the kennel that I inhabited); that I should die if I remained a month longer in that den; that all lodgings in St. Petersburg were detestable; and that he would be glad to know if I was in want of anything.

So thunderstruck was I with the proposal that I could only burst into tears. These tears he interpreted as a sign of gratitude, for he told me that he had always felt assured of my good sense, cleverness, and sensibility, but that hitherto he had hesitated to take this step until he should have learned precisely how I was getting on. Next he asked me some questions about YOU; saying that he had heard of you as a man of good principle, and that since he was unwilling to remain your debtor, would a sum of five hundred roubles repay you for all you had done for me? To this I replied that your services to myself had been such as could never be requited with money; whereupon, he exclaimed that I was talking rubbish and nonsense; that evidently I was still young enough to read poetry; that romances of this kind were the undoing of young girls, that books only corrupted morality, and that, for his part, he could not abide them. "You ought to live as long as I have done," he added, "and THEN you will see what men can be."

With that he requested me to give his proposal my favourable consideration—saying that he would not like me to take such an important step unguardedly, since want of thought and impetuosity often spelt ruin to youthful inexperience, but that he hoped to receive an answer in the affirmative. "Otherwise," said he, "I shall have no choice but to marry a certain merchant's daughter in Moscow, in order that I may keep my vow to deprive my nephew of the inheritance."—Then he pressed five hundred roubles into my hand—to buy myself some bonbons, as he phrased it—and wound up by saying that in the country I should grow as fat as a doughnut or a cheese rolled in butter; that at the present moment he was extremely busy; and that, deeply engaged in business though he had been all day, he had snatched the present opportunity of paying me a visit. At length he departed.

For a long time I sat plunged in reflection. Great though my distress of mind was, I soon arrived at a decision.... My friend, I am going to marry this man; I have no choice but to accept his proposal. If anyone could save me from this squalor, and restore to me my good name, and avert from me future poverty and want and misfortune, he is the man to do it. What else have I to look for from the future? What more am I to ask of fate? Thedora declares that one need NEVER lose one's happiness; but what, I ask HER, can be called happiness under such circumstances as mine? At all events I see no other road open, dear friend. I see nothing else to be done. I have worked until I have ruined my health. I cannot go on working forever. Shall I go out into the world? Nay; I am worn to a shadow with grief, and become good for nothing. Sickly by nature, I should merely be a burden upon other folks. Of course this marriage will not bring me paradise, but what else does there remain, my friend—what else does there remain? What other choice is left?

I had not asked your advice earlier for the reason that I wanted to think the matter over alone. However, the decision which you have just read is unalterable, and I am about to announce it to Bwikov himself, who in any case has pressed me for a speedy reply, owing to the fact (so he says) that his business will not wait nor allow him to remain here longer, and that therefore, no trifle must be allowed to stand in its way. God alone knows whether I shall be happy, but my fate is in His holy, His inscrutable hand, and I have so decided. Bwikov is said to be kind-hearted. He will at least respect me, and perhaps I shall be able to return that respect. What more could be looked for from such a marriage?

I have now told you all, Makar Alexievitch, and feel sure that you will understand my despondency. Do not, however, try to divert me from my intention, for all your efforts will be in vain. Think for a moment; weigh in your heart for a moment all that has led me to take this step. At first my anguish was extreme, but now I am quieter. What awaits me I know not. What must be must be, and as God may send....

Bwikov has just arrived, so I am leaving this letter unfinished. Otherwise I had much else to say to you. Bwikov is even now at the door!...

September 23rd

MY BELOVED BARBARA ALEXIEVNA—I hasten to reply to you—I hasten to express to you my extreme astonishment.... In passing, I may mention that yesterday we buried poor Gorshkov....

Yes, Bwikov has acted nobly, and you have no choice but to accept him. All things are in God's hands. This is so, and must always be so; and the purposes of the Divine Creator are at once good and inscrutable, as also is Fate, which is one with Him....

Thedora will share your happiness—for, of course, you will be happy, and free from want, darling, dearest, sweetest of angels! But why should the matter be so hurried? Oh, of course—Monsieur Bwikov's business affairs. Only a man who has no affairs to see to can afford to disregard such things. I got a glimpse of Monsieur Bwikov as he was leaving your door. He is a fine-looking man—a very fine-looking man; though that is not the point that I should most have noticed had I been quite myself at the time....

In the future shall we be able to write letters to one another? I keep wondering and wondering what has led you to say all that you have said. To think that just when twenty pages of my copying are completed THIS has happened!... I suppose you will be able to make many purchases now—to buy shoes and dresses and all sorts of things? Do you remember the shops in Gorokhovaia Street of which I used to speak?...

But no. You ought not to go out at present—you simply ought not to, and shall not. Presently, you will he able to buy many, many things, and to, keep a carriage. Also, at present the weather is bad. Rain is descending in pailfuls, and it is such a soaking kind of rain that—that you might catch cold from it, my darling, and the chill might go to your heart. Why should your fear of this man lead you to take such risks when all the time I am here to do your bidding? So Thedora declares great happiness to be awaiting you, does she? She is a gossiping old woman, and evidently desires to ruin you.

Shall you be at the all-night Mass this evening, dearest? I should like to come and see you there. Yes, Bwikov spoke but the truth when he said that you are a woman of virtue, wit, and good feeling. Yet I think he would do far better to marry the merchant's daughter. What think YOU about it? Yes, 'twould be far better for him. As soon as it grows dark tonight I mean to come and sit with you for an hour. Tonight twilight will close in early, so I shall soon be with you. Yes, come what may, I mean to see you for an hour. At present, I suppose, you are expecting Bwikov, but I will come as soon as he has gone. So stay at home until I have arrived, dearest.

MAKAR DIEVUSHKIN.

September 27th

DEAR MAKAR ALEXIEVITCH—Bwikov has just informed me that I must have at least three dozen linen blouses; so I must go at once and look for sempstresses to make two out of the three dozen, since time presses. Indeed, Monsieur Bwikov is quite angry about the fuss which these fripperies are entailing, seeing that there remain but five days before the wedding, and we are to depart on the following day. He keeps rushing about and declaring that no time ought to be wasted on trifles. I am terribly worried, and scarcely able to stand on my feet. There is so much to do, and, perhaps, so much that were better left undone! Moreover, I have no blond or other lace; so THERE is another item to be purchased, since Bwikov declares that he cannot have his bride look like a cook, but, on the contrary, she must "put the noses of the great ladies out of joint." That is his expression. I wish, therefore, that you would go to Madame Chiffon's, in Gorokhovaia Street, and ask her, in the first place, to send me some sempstresses, and, in the second place, to give herself the trouble of coming in person, as I am too ill to go out. Our new flat is very cold, and still in great disorder. Also, Bwikov has an aunt who is at her last gasp through old age, and may die before our departure. He himself, however, declares this to be nothing, and says that she will soon recover. He is not yet living with me, and I have to go running hither and thither to find him. Only Thedora is acting as my servant, together with Bwikov's valet, who oversees everything, but has been absent for the past three days.

Each morning Bwikov goes to business, and loses his temper. Yesterday he even had some trouble with the police because of his thrashing the steward of these buildings... I have no one to send with this letter so I am going to post it... Ah! I had almost forgotten the most important point—which is that I should like you to go and tell Madame Chiffon that I wish the blond lace to be changed in conformity with yesterday's patterns, if she will be good enough to bring with her a new assortment. Also say that I have altered my mind about the satin, which I wish to be tamboured with crochet-work; also, that tambour is to be used with monograms on the various garments. Do you hear? Tambour, not smooth work. Do not forget that it is to be tambour. Another thing I had almost forgotten, which is that the lappets of the fur cloak must be raised, and the collar bound with lace. Please tell her these things, Makar Alexievitch.—Your friend,

B. D.

P.S.—I am so ashamed to trouble you with my commissions! This is the third morning that you will have spent in running about for my sake. But what else am I to do? The whole place is in disorder, and I myself am ill. Do not be vexed with me, Makar Alexievitch. I am feeling so depressed! What is going to become of me, dear friend, dear, kind, old Makar Alexievitch? I dread to look forward into the future. Somehow I feel apprehensive; I am living, as it were, in a mist. Yet, for God's sake, forget none of my commissions. I am so afraid lest you should make a mistake! Remember that everything is to be tambour work, not smooth.

September 27th

MY BELOVED BARBARA ALEXIEVNA—I have carefully fulfilled your commissions. Madame Chiffon informs me that she herself had thought of using tambour work as being more suitable (though I did not quite take in all she said). Also, she has informed me that, since you have given certain directions in writing, she has followed them (though again I do not clearly remember all that she said—I only remember that she said a very great deal, for she is a most tiresome old woman). These observations she will soon be repeating to you in person. For myself, I feel absolutely exhausted, and have not been to the office today...

Do not despair about the future, dearest. To save you trouble I would visit every shop in St. Petersburg. You write that you dare not look forward into the future. But by tonight, at seven o'clock, you will have learned all, for Madame Chiffon will have arrived in person to see you. Hope on, and everything will order itself for the best. Of course, I am referring only to these accursed gewgaws, to these frills and fripperies! Ah me, ah me, how glad I shall be to see you, my angel! Yes, how glad I shall be! Twice already today I have passed the gates of your abode. Unfortunately, this Bwikov is a man of such choler that—Well, things are as they are.

MAKAR DIEVUSHKIN.

September 28th

MY DEAREST MAKAR ALEXIEVITCH—For God's sake go to the jeweller's, and tell him that, after all, he need not make the pearl and emerald earrings. Monsieur Bwikov says that they will cost him too much, that they will burn a veritable hole in his pocket. In fact, he has lost his temper again, and declares that he is being robbed. Yesterday he added that, had he but known, but foreseen, these expenses, he would never have married. Also, he says that, as things are, he intends only to have a plain wedding, and then to depart. "You must not look for any dancing or festivity or entertainment of guests, for our gala times are still in the air." Such were his words. God knows I do not want such things, but none the less Bwikov has forbidden them. I made him no answer on the subject, for he is a man all too easily irritated. What, what is going to become of me?

B. D.

September 28th

MY BELOVED BARBARA ALEXIEVNA—All is well as regards the jeweller. Unfortunately, I have also to say that I myself have fallen ill, and cannot rise from bed. Just when so many things need to be done, I have gone and caught a chill, the devil take it! Also I have to tell you that, to complete my misfortunes, his Excellency has been pleased to become stricter. Today he railed at and scolded Emelia Ivanovitch until the poor fellow was quite put about. That is the sum of my news.

No—there is something else concerning which I should like to write to you, but am afraid to obtrude upon your notice. I am a simple, dull fellow who writes down whatsoever first comes into his head— Your friend,

MAKAR DIEVUSHKIN.

September 29th

MY OWN BARBARA ALEXIEVNA—Today, dearest, I saw Thedora, who informed me that you are to be married tomorrow, and on the following day to go away—for which purpose Bwikov has ordered a post-chaise....

Well, of the incident of his Excellency, I have already told you. Also I have verified the bill from the shop in Gorokhovaia Street. It is correct, but very long. Why is Monsieur Bwikov so out of humour with you? Nay, but you must be of good cheer, my darling. I am so, and shall always be so, so long as you are happy. I should have come to the church tomorrow, but, alas, shall be prevented from doing so by the pain in my loins. Also, I would have written an account of the ceremony, but that there will be no one to report to me the details....

Yes, you have been a very good friend to Thedora, dearest. You have acted kindly, very kindly, towards her. For every such deed God will bless you. Good deeds never go unrewarded, nor does virtue ever fail to win the crown of divine justice, be it early or be it late. Much else should I have liked to write to you. Every hour, every minute I could occupy in writing. Indeed I could write to you forever! Only your book, "The Stories of Bielkin", is left to me. Do not deprive me of it, I pray you, but suffer me to keep it. It is not so much because I wish to read the book for its own sake, as because winter is coming on, when the evenings will be long and dreary, and one will want to read at least SOMETHING.

Do you know, I am going to move from my present quarters into your old ones, which I intend to rent from Thedora; for I could never part with that good old woman. Moreover, she is such a splendid worker. Yesterday I inspected your empty room in detail, and inspected your embroidery-frame, with the work still hanging on it. It had been left untouched in its corner. Next, I inspected the work itself, of which there still remained a few remnants, and saw that you had used one of my letters for a spool upon which to wind your thread. Also, on the table I found a scrap of paper which had written on it, "My dearest Makar Alexievitch I hasten to—" that was all. Evidently, someone had interrupted you at an interesting point. Lastly, behind a screen there was your little bed.... Oh darling of darlings!!!... Well, goodbye now, goodbye now, but for God's sake send me something in answer to this letter!

MAKAR DIEVUSHKIN.

September 30th

MY BELOVED MAKAR ALEXIEVITCH—All is over! The die is cast! What my lot may have in store I know not, but I am submissive to the will of God. Tomorrow, then, we depart. For the last time, I take my leave of you, my friend beyond price, my benefactor, my dear one! Do not grieve for me, but try to live happily. Think of me sometimes, and may the blessing of Almighty God light upon you! For myself, I shall often have you in remembrance, and recall you in my prayers. Thus our time together has come to an end. Little comfort in my new life shall I derive from memories of the past. The more, therefore, shall I cherish the recollection of you, and the dearer will you ever be to my heart. Here, you have been my only friend; here, you alone have loved me. Yes, I have seen all, I have known all—I have throughout known how well you love me. A single smile of mine, a single stroke from my pen, has been able to make you happy.... But now you must forget me.... How lonely you will be! Why should you stay here at all, kind, inestimable, but solitary, friend of mine?

To your care I entrust the book, the embroidery frame, and the letter upon which I had begun. When you look upon the few words which the letter contains you will be able mentally to read in thought all that you would have liked further to hear or receive from me—all that I would so gladly have written, but can never now write. Think sometimes of your poor little Barbara who loved you so well. All your letters I have left behind me in the top drawer of Thedora's chest of drawers... You write that you are ill, but Monsieur Bwikov will not let me leave the house today; so that I can only write to you. Also, I will write again before long. That is a promise. Yet God only knows when I shall be able to do so....

Now we must bid one another forever farewell, my friend, my beloved, my own! Yes, it must be forever! Ah, how at this moment I could embrace you! Goodbye, dear friend—goodbye, goodbye! May you ever rest well and happy! To the end I shall keep you in my prayers. How my heart is aching under its load of sorrow!... Monsieur Bwikov is just calling for me....—Your ever loving

B.

P.S.—My heart is full! It is full to bursting of tears! Sorrow has me in its grip, and is tearing me to pieces. Goodbye. My God, what grief! Do not, do not forget your poor Barbara!

BELOVED BARBARA—MY JEWEL, MY PRICELESS ONE—You are now almost en route, you are now just about to depart! Would that they had torn my heart out of my breast rather than have taken you away from me! How could you allow it? You weep, yet you go! And only this moment I have received from you a letter stained with your tears! It must be that you are departing unwillingly; it must be that you are being abducted against your will; it must be that you are sorry for me; it must be that—that you LOVE me!...

Yet how will it fare with you now? Your heart will soon have become chilled and sick and depressed. Grief will soon have sucked away its life; grief will soon have rent it in twain! Yes, you will die where you be, and be laid to rest in the cold, moist earth where there is no one to bewail you. Monsieur Bwikov will only be hunting hares!...

Ah, my darling, my darling! WHY did you come to this decision? How could you bring yourself to take such a step? What have you done, have you done, have you done? Soon they will be carrying you away to the tomb; soon your beauty will have become defiled, my angel. Ah, dearest one, you are as weak as a feather. And where have I been all this time? What have I been thinking of? I have treated you merely as a forward child whose head was aching. Fool that I was, I neither saw nor understood. I have behaved as though, right or wrong, the matter was in no way my concern. Yes, I have been running about after fripperies!... Ah, but I WILL leave my bed. Tomorrow I WILL rise sound and well, and be once more myself....

Dearest, I could throw myself under the wheels of a passing vehicle rather than that you should go like this. By what right is it being done?... I will go with you; I will run behind your carriage if you will not take me—yes, I will run, and run so long as the power is in me, and until my breath shall have failed. Do you know whither you are going? Perhaps you will not know, and will have to ask me? Before you there lie the Steppes, my darling—only the Steppes, the naked Steppes, the Steppes that are as bare as the palm of my hand. THERE there live only heartless old women and rude peasants and drunkards. THERE the trees have already shed their leaves. THERE there abide but rain and cold. Why should you go thither? True, Monsieur Bwikov will have his diversions in that country—he will be able to hunt the hare; but what of yourself? Do you wish to become a mere estate lady? Nay; look at yourself, my seraph of heaven. Are you in any way fitted for such a role? How could you play it? To whom should I write letters? To whom should I send these missives? Whom should I call "my darling"? To whom should I apply that name of endearment? Where, too, could I find you?

When you are gone, Barbara, I shall die—for certain I shall die, for my heart cannot bear this misery. I love you as I love the light of God; I love you as my own daughter; to you I have devoted my love in its entirety; only for you have I lived at all; only because you were near me have I worked and copied manuscripts and committed my views to paper under the guise of friendly letters.

Perhaps you did not know all this, but it has been so. How, then, my beloved, could you bring yourself to leave me? Nay, you MUST not go—it is impossible, it is sheerly, it is utterly, impossible. The rain will fall upon you, and you are weak, and will catch cold. The floods will stop your carriage. No sooner will it have passed the city barriers than it will break down, purposely break down. Here, in St. Petersburg, they are bad builders of carriages. Yes, I know well these carriage-builders. They are jerry-builders who can fashion a toy, but nothing that is durable. Yes, I swear they can make nothing that is durable.... All that I can do is to go upon my knees before Monsieur Bwikov, and to tell him all, to tell him all. Do you also tell him all, dearest, and reason with him. Tell him that you MUST remain here, and must not go. Ah, why did he not marry that merchant's daughter in Moscow? Let him go and marry her now. She would suit him far better and for reasons which I well know. Then I could keep you. For what is he to you, this Monsieur Bwikov? Why has he suddenly become so dear to your heart? Is it because he can buy you gewgaws? What are THEY? What use are THEY? They are so much rubbish. One should consider human life rather than mere finery.

Nevertheless, as soon as I have received my next instalment of salary I mean to buy you a new cloak. I mean to buy it at a shop with which I am acquainted. Only, you must wait until my next installment is due, my angel of a Barbara. Ah, God, my God! To think that you are going away into the Steppes with Monsieur Bwikov—that you are going away never to return!... Nay, nay, but you SHALL write to me. You SHALL write me a letter as soon as you have started, even if it be your last letter of all, my dearest. Yet will it be your last letter? How has it come about so suddenly, so irrevocably, that this letter should be your last? Nay, nay; I will write, and you shall write—yes, NOW, when at length I am beginning to improve my style. Style? I do not know what I am writing. I never do know what I am writing. I could not possibly know, for I never read over what I have written, nor correct its orthography. At the present moment, I am writing merely for the sake of writing, and to put as much as possible into this last letter of mine....

Ah, dearest, my pet, my own darling!...

Fyodor Dostoyevsky was born on 11th November 1821, the second child of Dr. Mikhail Dostoyevsky and Maria Dostoeskaya (neé Nechayeva).

His early years were spent at the family home in the grounds of the Mariinsky Hospital for the Poor, located in a lower-class district at the edge of Moscow. Here Dostoyevsky encountered the patients when playing in the hospital gardens.

He was introduced to literature very early. At age three, it was heroic sagas, fairy tales and legends. At four his mother used the Bible to teach him to read and write. His immersion in literature was wide and varied; the Russian writers Karamzin, Pushkin and Derzhavin; Gothic fiction such as Ann Radcliffe; romantic works by Schiller and Goethe; heroic tales by Cervantes and Walter Scott; and Homer's epics. His imagination, he later recalled, was brought to life by his parents' nightly readings.

Although Dostoyevsky had a delicate physical constitution, his parents thought him as hot-headed, stubborn and cheeky.

In 1833, his very religious father, sent him to a French boarding school and then the Chermak boarding school. Dostoyevsky was described as a pale, introverted dreamer but also an over-excitable romantic. He felt out of place among his aristocratic classmates but the experiences would be useful in his later writing.

On 27th September 1837 tragedy struck. Dostoyevsky's mother died of tuberculosis

Dostoyevsky and his brother were now enrolled at the Nikolayev Military Engineering Institute, their academic studies abandoned for military careers. Mikhail, on health grounds, was refused admission and sent to the Academy in Reval, Estonia.

Dostoyevsky disliked the academy and its pursuit of science, mathematics and military engineering. His interests were drawing and architecture. He became an outsider among his 120 classmates. However his bravery and a strong sense of justice meant respect from his fellow students although he was solitary and sought refuge in his own literary world.

His father died on 16th June 1839 and some accounts say the event triggered Dostoyevsky's epilepsy. However, he continued his studies, passed his exams and obtained the rank of engineer cadet, allowing him to live outside the academy. He visited Mikhail in Reval, and frequently attended concerts, operas, plays, ballets and was also introduced to a love of gambling.

Dostoyevsky's first completed work was a translation of Honoré de Balzac's novel Eugénie Grandet. It was published in mid-1843 in the journal Repertoire and Pantheon. Other translations followed but none were successful. He believed his financial difficulties could be overcome by writing his own novel.

He completed 'Poor Folk' in May 1845. It was published in 1846 in the St Petersburg Collection almanac and was a commercial success. It was described by the influential literary critic Vissarion Belinsky as Russia's first "social novel".

Dostoyevsky felt that his military career would curtail his flourishing literary career and so resigned his post. His next novel, 'The Double', initially appeared in the journal Notes of the Fatherland in January 1846. Dostoyevsky now became immersed, through the writings of Cabet, Proudhon and Saint-Simon in socialism. He was attracted to the logic, sense of justice and its devotion to those of lesser means.

'The Double' received bad reviews resulting in a deterioration in Dostoyevsky's health, mainly through more frequent seizures, but he continued to write. Between 1846-1848 several short stories were published including 'Mr. Prokharchin', 'The Landlady', 'A Weak Heart', and 'White Nights' but none were popular. With his debts mounting he joined the utopian socialist Betekov circle, a tightly knit community which helped him to survive. When that dissolved he joined the Petrashevsky Circle, which proposed social reforms in Russia. Dostoyevsky used the circle's library at weekends and occasionally joined their discussions on freedom and the abolition of serfdom.

The Petrashevsky Circle was denounced to the Ministry of Internal Affairs and Dostoyevsky himself accused of reading and distributing banned works. The members were arrested on 23rd April 1849.

Inconveniently at this time the first parts of 'Netochka Nezvanova', were published in Annals of the Fatherland, but his banishment ended the project. Dostoyevsky never attempted to finish it.

His case was discussed for four months by an investigative commission. The sentence was death by firing squad. The Tsar commuted the sentence to four years of exile with hard labour at a prison camp in Omsk, Siberia, followed by a term of compulsory military service.

Classified as a dangerous convict, Dostoyevsky had his hands and feet shackled until his release. He was only permitted to read his New Testament Bible. His health once more declined.

On his release in February 1854, Dostoyevsky asked Mikhail to help him financially and to send him books. In mid-March he moved to Semipalatinsk, where he was forced to serve in the Siberian Army Corps of the Seventh Line Battalion.

In Semipalatinsk, Dostoyevsky tutored several schoolchildren and met the family of Alexander and Maria Isaeva. He fell in love with her. Isaev was then posted to Kuznetsk, where he died in August 1855. Maria and her son then moved with Dostoyevsky to Barnaul.

In 1856 Dostoyevsky sent a letter apologising for his previous activities. As a result, he was allowed to publish books and to marry, although he remained under police surveillance his whole life. Maria married Dostoyevsky in Semipalatinsk on 7th February 1857, though she was worried about his poor financial situation. Their family life was unhappy and she found it difficult to cope with his health issues.

Dostoyevsky continued to write and be published though his income was thin. His writings on his prison experiences, 'Notes from the House of the Dead' was published in Russky Mir in September 1860. 'The Insulted and the Injured' appeared in the new Vremya magazine, which had been set up with funds from his brother's cigarette factory.

Dostoyevsky travelled to western Europe for the first time in June 1862, visiting Cologne, Berlin, Dresden, Wiesbaden, Belgium, Paris and London. He travelled with Nikolay Strakhov (who he worked with at both the Time and Epoch periodicals) through Switzerland and several North Italian cities. He recorded his impressions in 'Winter Notes on Summer Impressions', and also took time to criticize capitalism, social modernisation, materialism, Catholicism and Protestantism.

In August 1863, Dostoyevsky made another trip to Paris and met Polina Suslova and they developed a tempestuous relationship. He also lost almost all of his funds gambling in Wiesbaden and Baden-Baden. In 1864 his wife Maria and brother Mikhail died, and Dostoyevsky became the lone parent of his stepson Pasha and the sole support to his brother's family. The failure of Epoch, the magazine he had founded with Mikhail after Vremya was suppressed, worsened his finances, although with the help of relatives and friends he staved off bankruptcy.

The first two parts of his masterpiece 'Crime and Punishment' were published in early 1866 in The Russian Messenger periodical.

Dostoyevsky returned to Saint Petersburg in mid-September and promised his editor he would complete 'The Gambler', a short novel on gambling addiction, by November, although work on it had not yet begun. A friend advised him to hire a secretary and Dostoyevsky hired the twenty-year-old Anna Grigoryevna Snitkina. Her shorthand helped Dostoyevsky to complete 'The Gambler' in just 26 days.

On 15th February 1867 Dostoyevsky married Snitkina in Trinity Cathedral, Saint Petersburg. The 7,000 rubles he had earned from 'Crime and Punishment' did not cover his debts, forcing Anna to sell her valuables. On 14th April 1867, they began a honeymoon in Germany, staying in Berlin and Dresden, where he sought inspiration for his writing. They continued through Frankfurt, Darmstadt, Heidelberg and Karlsruhe. They spent five weeks in Baden-Baden, where Dostoyevsky quarreled with Turgenev and again lost much money at the roulette table. Then on to Geneva.

In September 1867, Dostoyevsky began work on 'The Idiot'. After a prolonged planning process he managed to write the first 100 pages in only 23 days; the serialisation began in The Russian Messenger in January 1868.

Their first child, Sonya was born in Geneva in March 1868 but died of pneumonia three months later. Anna recalled how Dostoyevsky "wept and sobbed like a woman in despair". The couple moved from Geneva to Vevey and then Milan and finally Florence. 'The Idiot' was completed there with the final part appearing in February 1869. Anna gave birth to their second daughter, Lyubov, in September 1869 in Dresden. In April 1871, Dostoyevsky made a final visit to a gambling hall in Wiesbaden. Anna claimed that he stopped gambling after the birth of their second daughter.

After hearing that the socialist revolutionary group "People's Vengeance" had murdered one of its own members Dostoyevsky began writing 'Demons'.

Back in Russia their son Fyodor was born on 16th July. They hoped to cancel their debts by selling their rental house in Peski, but tenant difficulties meant a low selling price, and disputes with their creditors continued. Anna suggested that they raise money on her husband's copyrights and pay off their debts in installments.

'Demons' was finished in November and published in January 1873 by the "Dostoyevsky Publishing Company". Anna managed the finances. They only accepted payment in cash and the bookshop was in their own apartment but the book was a success, and they sold around 3,000 copies. Dostoyevsky now proposed a periodical to be called A Writer's Diary. But funds were in short supply and so the Diary was published in Vladimir Meshchersky's The Citizen, beginning on 1st January, in return for an annual salary of 3,000 rubles.

In March 1874, Dostoyevsky left The Citizen because of the stress and interference from the Russian bureaucracy.

He offered to sell a new novel that he had not yet begun to write to The Russian Messenger, but they declined. Nikolay Nekrasov suggested that he publish 'A Writer's Diary' in Notes of the Fatherland; at 250 rubles for each printer's sheet - 100 more than he received from The Russian Messenger. Dostoyevsky accepted. As his health declined, he consulted doctors in St Petersburg and was told to take a cure outside Russia. In Ems he was diagnosed with acute catarrh. He now began work on 'The Adolescent'.

Anna proposed that they spend the winter in Staraya Russa to allow Dostoyevsky to rest. On 10th August 1875 his son Alexey was born.

Dostoyevsky finished 'The Adolescent' at the end of 1875, although once more it was serialised in Notes of the Fatherland as he wrote.

In early 1876, Dostoyevsky continued work on his Diary. The collection sold more than twice as many copies as his previous books. With assistance from Anna's brother, the family bought a dacha in Staraya Russa. In the summer of 1876, Dostoyevsky began experiencing shortness of breath again. He once more visited Ems and was told that he might live another 15 years if he moved to a healthier climate. When he returned to Russia, Tsar Alexander II ordered Dostoyevsky to visit his palace to present the Diary to him, and 'requested' that he educate his sons, Sergey and Paul.

Dostoyevsky's health continued to decline, and in March 1877 he had four epileptic seizures.

He was appointed an honorary member of the Russian Academy of Sciences, in February 1879. On 16th May his son Alyosha had a severe epileptic seizure and died.

In the summer of 1879 he was elected to the honorary committee of the Association Littéraire et Artistique Internationale, whose members included Victor Hugo, Ivan Turgenev, Alfred Tennyson, Anthony Trollope, Henry Longfellow, Ralph Waldo Emerson and Leo Tolstoy.

Dostoyevsky made a final visit to Ems in early August 1879. He was diagnosed with early-stage pulmonary emphysema. He was told it could be successfully managed, but not cured.

On 3rd February 1880 Dostoyevsky was elected vice-president of the Slavic Benevolent Society, and invited to speak at the unveiling of the Pushkin memorial in Moscow. On 8th June he delivered an impressive speech. It was met with an ovation. Even his long-time rival Turgenev embraced him.

On 26th January 1881 Dostoyevsky suffered a pulmonary haemorrhage. After another Anna called the doctors, who gave a poor prognosis. A third haemorrhage followed shortly afterwards.

Fyodor Dostoyevsky died on 9th February, 1881. His body was placed on a table, following Russian custom. He was interred in the Tikhvin Cemetery at the Alexander Nevsky Convent, near his favourite poets, Nikolay Karamzin and Vasily Zhukovsky.

It is unclear how many attended his funeral though many accounts say it was in the tens of thousands.

Fyodor Dostoyevsky – A Concise Bibliography

Novels and novellas
Poor Folk (novella) (1846)
The Double (novella) (1846)
The Landlady (novella) (1847)
Netochka Nezvanova (unfinished) (1849)
Uncle's Dream (novella) (1859)
The Village of Stepanchikovo (1859)
The Insulted and The Injured aka Humiliated and Insulted (1861)
The House of the Dead (1862)
Notes from Underground (novella) (1864)
Crime and Punishment (1866)
The Gambler (novella) (1867)
The Idiot (1869)
The Eternal Husband (novella) aka The Permanent Husband (1870)
Demons (aka The Possessed, The Devils) (1872)
The Adolescent (1875)
The Brothers Karamazov (1880)

Short Stories

Mr. Prokharchin (1846)
Novel in Nine Letters (1847)
Another Man's Wife and a Husband under the Bed (merger of Another Man's Wife and A Jealous Husband) (1848)
A Weak Heart (1848)
Polzunkov (1848)
An Honest Thief (1848)
A Christmas Tree and a Wedding (1848)
White Nights (1848)
A Little Hero (1849)
A Nasty Story (1862)
The Crocodile (1865)
Bobok (1873)
The Heavenly Christmas Tree (aka The Beggar Boy at Christ's Christmas Tree) (1876)
A Gentle Creature (1876)
The Peasant Marey (1876)

The Dream of a Ridiculous Man (1877)

Essay Collections

Winter Notes on Summer Impressions (1863)
A Writer's Diary (1873–1881)

Translations

Eugénie Grandet (Honoré de Balzac) (1843)
La dernière Aldini (George Sand) (1843)
Mary Stuart (Friedrich Schiller) (1843)
Boris Godunov (Alexander Pushkin) (1843)

Personal letters

Letters of Fyodor Michailovitch Dostoyevsky to His Family and Friends by Fyodor Mikhailovich Dostoyevsky (Author), translator Ethel Colburn (1912)

Posthumously Published Notebooks

Stavrogin's Confession & the Plan of the Life of a Great Sinner – English translation by Virginia Woolf and S. S. Koteliansky (1922)